Courting Her Monsters

The Monsters You Know
Book 1
Erin Bedford

Cover Design by Atlantis Book Design

Editing by Makenzie Frazier

Also by Erin Bedford

Courting Her Monsters

The Monsters You Know
Book 1
Erin Bedford

Chapter 1

THE WHOLE FLOOR VIBRATED BENEATH my feet. My desk bounced beneath my hands and my glass of water inches from my hand rippled with each stomp of whoever was running down the hall. When the vibration stopped, I let out a breath, returning my eyes to my letter, the quill flipping over and over in between my fingers.

Where was I?

Lady Rosemary wanted me to come to her garden party tomorrow after lunch. My nose wrinkled. While the lady in question wasn't horrible company, her friends could be difficult to deal with. Many of them purposely do not include me in their conversations. It made me wonder why they even bothered to invite me.

Just as I placed my quill to the paper, the whole table shook violently. My quill slipped leaving a long line of ink off the page. Scowling, I twisted in my seat to glare at the person who had slammed my door shut.

My handmaiden, Aryn, bent at the waist, her hands on her knees and her shoulders coming up and down with each breath she took. I waited for her to catch her breath and took in the pale pallor of her complexion. Something must have happened to cause my usually calm minded handmaiden to come rushing to my room.

Her throat visibly swallowed as she slowly stood at her full five-foot three height, her shoulders back and nose going slightly into the air as if that would make up for her abrupt entrance. Her mouth opened as her hands began to move before her.

"Your highness," she swallowed and licked her lips, "they're here." The aggressiveness of her hand movements showed exactly how Aryn felt about our visitors.

I could hardly blame her.

Today was the day I met my betrothed. The man my father deemed I would marry to bring our two kingdoms together. I always knew I'd have to marry for the good of the kingdom. Especially as the sole heir to the King of Kinokos. My father would want me to marry well and that time seemed to be coming quickly upon us.

Pushing my correspondence to the side, I stood from my chair and smoothed my hands down the pale blue of my gown. I applaud myself for having the forethought to wear a receiving gown today rather than my usual day gown. While I wasn't sure my betrothal's party would arrive today, I had wanted to be prepared in case they did.

"Let's get this over with," I answered with my hands.

Aryn opened the door for me, following alongside me as we moved down the hallway toward the receiving hall. Several servants signed hello and good afternoon to me and I nodded in return, trying my best not to seem nervous for the coming encounter.

When we arrived at the last turn to head downstairs, Aryn placed a hand on my arm, stopping me.

"What is it?" my hand movements more aggressive than I wanted them to be, giving away how turbulent I was feeling inside.

Aryn's face softened. "Your mother would be so proud of you."

My eyes welled up at the mention of my mother. She'd died not three years ago from the same sickness that had taken my hearing. Some days I wished it had taken me too. Today was one of those days. "I wish she was here."

Aryn squeezed my arm with a small smile. "Me too." She placed a hand to the center of her chest and then made a heart with her fingers placing it to her left breast.

A watery smile covered my face as I returned the sign.

Aryn had been my mother's handmaiden before she died. When she passed Aryn took it upon herself to watch over me in my mother's place. She had been who I clung to those first few months of learning to hear all over again. While I still had my voice, learning to become aware of others by their movements and then learning to use this strange hand language was another challenge all on its own. Several years later, I found that I could learn far more about what the person was saying from what I wasn't hearing than from what I could have learned through their words.

I also found out who my real friends were during that time. Those who wanted to stay at my side worked to learn my new way of speaking and hearing while others distanced themselves. Too uncomfortable to be near me any longer. Who needed them anyway?

"Come," Aryn patted my back, ushering me forward. "Let's not keep your handsome prince waiting."

I laughed at the silly face she made at the word prince.

Handsome was far down on the line of desires on my checklist for a husband. While attractiveness is a bonus, there were far more other qualities in my betrothed that I was looking for. Kindness for one. Understanding. Patience. A willingness to listen, not just to the sound of his own voice but to those around him. Even when they aren't speaking.

I admitted it was wishful thinking on my part. The most I could hope for from the prince of Plumus — a kingdom known for their waterways, sea trades, and aggressive negotiations — was not to dismiss me as stupid for being broken.

Some would say I was lucky that Calahan even considered marrying someone like me. To those I had a vulgar gesture they could shove up their asses. I had thoughts and feelings just the same

11

as before I lost my hearing — if even more so than before.

My fingers trailed along the railing of the stairs, the sweat from my hand slickening the wood beneath my palm. Each step beneath my feet was heavy and I forced myself to take a breath and make my steps as light as a feather. I didn't want them to think I was uncivilized as well as broken.

The hair on my bare forearms prickled with each step closer to the receiving room. Small vibrations moved through the air toward me. It had been quite an unusual experience to find myself feeling more than hearing people talk. While I may not know what they were saying, I could pick up the timber of their voice and the amount of them by how much the air shifted. I didn't think that my other senses had enhanced with the loss of one. I tasted everything the same. However, my eyes noticed far more than before and I felt things I would never have noticed had my world not turned to silence.

When we arrived in the room, the speaking stopped and my father turned to me with a wide grin. "Here is my lovely daughter now." My father moved his hands with the words though he always made sure to speak clearly and slowly so I could read his lips. I appreciated his gestures regardless.

Stepping over to him, I embraced him, placing a kiss to his cheek before greeting him. "Good morning, father."

His hands still on my shoulders, my father turned me toward the men waiting patiently before us. His words vibrated against my face as he spoke. My gaze watched Aryn who interpreted the words for me when I could not see the speaker's mouth. "Cal, this is my daughter, Georgia."

My eyes shifted over to our visitors. The first man stood straight with his hands behind his back, his shoulders pulled back showing his well defined muscles through the dark red traveling shirt. His pants were beige with a bit of dirt here and there. And yet he didn't seem bothered by it. Good, someone who didn't mind getting their hands dirty. I didn't need any prim and proper prince who would squeal at the slightest fleck of dirt. Once I took in his body, taking note that his feet pointed toward myself and not my father, I allowed my eyes to raise to the face of the man I was to marry.

A strong jawline, covered with dark hair on most of his lower face. His full lips were encircled by hair as well. I didn't particularly care for facial hair. I could only be thankful he kept his beard trimmed and not scraggly and overgrown as some men did. My gaze lifted to a standard nose and a pair of pale blue eyes, lined with long dark lashes. They were eyes any woman could get lost in. They crinkled at the sides the longer I stared.

My father's hands squeezed on my shoulders and I realized the man had said something. Dropping my eyes to his mouth, I watched as his mouth formed the words, "I could not be more thrilled to meet you, princess. Or shall I say, wife?"

Giving him a polite smile, I swept into a curtsey. "It is a pleasure to meet you."

I did not lower my gaze as was customary when curtseying so I could see his mouth. Cal might be happy to see me but he made no effort to learn to speak to me easier by learning the hand gestures we all used here. I could have forgiven that had he only just known of me recently. As it were, Cal had known about our betrothal for most of a year and about my condition the whole time. In that time frame, one would think that he would have taken the time to learn at least the rudimentary signs.

"Good, you can speak." Cal spoke quickly, and I had to slide my eyes over to Cal every few moments to make sure I was understanding him right. "This is my brother, Luis." He clapped his hand on the shoulder of the man next to him. "I hope you will become as close with him as you and I am sure to be."

The twinkle in Cal's eyes at those words made me itch all over. I pushed it aside as jitters and curtsied to the other man. Luis was not as handsome as Cal. However, they had the same coloring and build. His eyes were more green than blue and his hair was a shade darker than Cal's. His clothing was perfectly pristine. Not at all like his brother.

Inclining his head, Luis held out a hand toward me. Unsure what he wished, I gave him my hand. His hands were smooth and cold, a bit sweaty and I forced myself not to cringe and jerk back my hand. He pressed a kiss to my knuckles. The slight pressure of his lips shouldn't have made my stomach roll and yet it did. I tried my best to withdraw my hand at a normal pace and not wipe in on the skirt of my gown.

"I hope to become quite close with my new sister." Luis surprised me by using the hand gestures as well as speaking. Well, at least one of them had made the effort.

Cal threw an arm around his brother's shoulders and laughed. "Always the overachiever." Then he turned his face away from me, to whisper something in his brother's ear that had the other stiffening.

I stepped back from them and into my father's warm embrace. To my father, I said aloud as well with my hands, "Why don't we allow our guests to freshen up in their rooms and perhaps have tea in thirty?" I turned the words toward my betrothed and his brother as well, cocking a brow at them.

"A fine idea." My father beamed at me and waved a hand toward a nearby servant. "Show our guests to their rooms and have the cook prepare something in the receiving room."

The servant stepped forward to assist as Cal waved him off, his mouth moving quickly.

I squinted at his lips, trying to keep up with his words, catching only every other one and having to put the sentence together myself.

"No need. I'd much prefer my soon to be wife to show me around, would you?"

I stilled at his question, unsure if I should. A glance at my father, told me to do it. I nodded and swept my skirts across the floor, leading the way up the stairs. Aryn began to follow us but Cal stopped her. Pausing on the steps with my hand on the railing, I watched with curious and cautious eyes.

Cal said something to her that I didn't see and Aryn didn't interpret for me. However, the look on her face said everything I needed to know. She was not happy with my new betrothed.

Cal continued up the stairs with Aryn lingering behind with his brother. Confused as to why he would wish her to stay behind, I turned and led him further into my home. We walked side by side for a few moments. A few servants passed up with curious looks, giving me a small bow of their heads on their way by. Some gestured a hello to me and a cautious one to Cal.

My eyes slid over to Cal's face every few moments, checking to see if he had decided to say something to me. Thankfully, he seemed perfectly happy walking in silence.

As we rounded a corner that led to the guest wing, Cal grabbed me by the elbow and swung me around until my back was pressed up against the wall of an alcove I liked to hide behind as a girl.

Not wanting to be rude and disappoint my father, I peered up at Cal with a frown. "Don't you want to see your room?" I voiced, unable to use my hands as he had them pinned down at my sides.

Cal smirked at me, lifting a hand to my face. He stroked a single finger along my cheek and then across my lips, pressing in enough that the tip scraped my teeth. "I wanted the chance to see what my wife has to offer."

My brows furrowed at his words. Had to offer? What in the world was he talking about? I was about to say as such when Cal lowered his face to my neck, his nose sliding along the column of it. He breathed in the scent of me as his hands found their way to the swell of my hips.

My back stiffened.

I was not unfamiliar with the ways of men. We were not some backward country that believed a woman was only worth something if she stayed intact. In fact, I'd had many lovers before I lost my hearing and even more so after. I was sure some of them had to do with the novelty of the idea, being with the princess, but even so, we had all left the encounter satisfied and happy.

Now however, with Cal sniffing me like a dog looking for a good place to piss, I wanted nothing but to have his hands and body as far away from me as possible.

His mouth moved along my exposed neck and shoulder, the words vibrated against my skin. I didn't know what he was saying and wasn't sure I wanted to know with the way his hands were sliding up my sides. I lifted my hands and pushed against his chest, giving him a slight nudge.

"We shouldn't be in here." I hoped my words would pull him out of whatever lust filled state he was in and make him come to his senses.

Cal's hands tightened on my sides almost to the point of hurting and he pressed his body flat against my own, grinding his hips against me so that I could feel how hard he was beneath his pants. He was speaking again. I knew he was and yet he never lifted his face so I could see what he said.

Seeing that I was getting nowhere with my betrothed, I grabbed a fist full of his hair and yanked it hard enough to get his attention. It did not have the desired effect.

Cal's lust filled eyes moved over my face and he licked his lips, this time speaking where I could understand him. "Oh, you are a feisty one. I'm going to enjoy breaking you."

Scowling, I shoved him back. "I may be your betrothed but I am not a whore you can just paw whenever you like. You will treat me with respect. Or I will be sure this marriage never happens."

Moving to get past him, I contemplated if I should tell my father what happened. I didn't get far before that hand was grabbing me again. Instead of shoving me against the wall this time, I found myself pressed up against the front of him. Cal twisted my arm behind my back until I bit my lip in pain. His other hand cupped my face, roughly turning it to see his own.

"This marriage will happen whether I fuck you here against the wall or on the table at dinner in front of your father. You know why?" His fingers tightened on my jaw. "Because your father needs me. He needs me so much that he's selling you off like the prized bitch you are and he'll let me do whatever I want to you as long as I give him my armies. My money. And you would do well to remember that fact. Without me, your little kingdom would be gone."

Part of me wished someone would come. That someone would see us and stop him. To my chagrin, I knew no one would. I picked this place to hide for a reason. No one would even know you existed standing here behind a rather large statue of one of my forefathers. Not unless they chose to look behind it, to see what was hidden in the shadows.

My experience told me I was on my own.

"You are a vile creature," I spat out, pushing against the hold he had on my arm only to have pain shoot through the joint.

Cal laughed before shoving his mouth against mine. His tongue ravished my mouth, almost making me gag. I bit down until I tasted blood. Cal shoved me away so hard that I hit the stone wall. I grappled for a hold on it, watching with blurry eyes as Cal used his thumb to wipe the blood from his lips. The grin he gave sent chills through my body, the blood coating his teeth and mouth making every word he said more vicious.

"This will be more fun than I thought."

Chapter 2

I SCRUBBED MY SKIN WITH the sponge until it turned red. The water was so hot that it almost scalded the flesh from my skin. It wasn't hot enough.

"Stop that." Aryn smacked my hands and signed, "You're hurting yourself."

I laughed. "I'm hurting myself?" I gestured at my body, signing with a vigilance. I showed her the marks that now marred my once unblemished skin. "I cannot hurt myself more than he has already done. I hate my skin. I hate his touch. I need to...I need to...get it off of me."

The wedding was coming closer and closer now. It was hard to imagine it had only been a few weeks since Cal and his vile brother had joined our court. It felt like an eternity. I tried my best to stay away from Cal. To find moments where I could hide away from him. He always found me.

It had become a game to him, to see how far he could push me before I could break and go to my father. I wouldn't though. I'd never go. He had made it perfectly clear what would happen if I did. I didn't know how bad it was, how close we were to falling apart. My father had done a good job of hiding it from me.

After my first encounter with Cal I had made it my duty to find out what my father had been keeping from me. I hunted through his study searching for any sign of what Cal had said was true and found ledgers of red, reports from the troops in the east of starvation and attacks from bordering kingdoms to the west. They knew how fragile and weak we were and they were closing in on us.

No wonder my father sought out an alliance with the most brutal of allies.

Cal was right. A marriage between our families would save the kingdom. Save my people. If I could survive that long.

"I do not know why you don't tell your father," Aryn shook her head and signed fiercely. "It's not right. What you let him do to you." The pity and sadness in her eyes only made me want to throw up.

I threw my sponge down with so much force that it bounced off the edge of the tub. "I can't. If he knew, then he'd stop the wedding."

Aryn held out a towel for me. "Isn't that what you want?"

I swallowed down my answer. More than anything. I never wanted to see Cal's face again. Never wanted to feel his touch on my skin or that of his brother's who he let touch me as freely as he liked as long as Cal was there to enjoy it too. His brother, Lu, was the worst of the two.

While Cal preferred to demean me and make me feel broken and useless, Lu wanted my pain. He liked knives in particular and as long as he didn't mar my pretty face as Cal put it, he had free reign over my body. The first time I'd felt the kiss of his blade, I thought I would never stop screaming. My throat had turned raw and hurt almost as much as the sharp edge digging into my flesh, carving out pieces of me until there was nothing left but them.

Aryn placed a hand on my arm. "Georgia."

I gave her a small watery smile. "No. We cannot end the engagement. Not until we figure something else out to save our people."

"That's not for you to figure out." Aryn jerked the curtain separating the tub from the rest of my bathing chamber back. "Your father is king. He needs to know what's happening to his daughter."

"Do you think it would make a difference?" I jerked the towel off my body, dropping it to the floor. "If we tell him and he breaks the engagement then we are still at the mercy of the other countries attacking in the west."

"You don't even know if that's true." Aryn gestured with rapid movements. "What enemies? Who is attacking us? Why don't we have any more money? These are all questions we need to know the answers to."

"How exactly am I going to get those answers? No one will tell me anything." I jerked my dress on over my body, wincing slightly as the material brushed against the newest marks on my skin. The newest reminder that I belonged to Cal and I was helpless to do anything about it.

Or so my betrothed thought.

Aryn was right. I couldn't just continue to do nothing. I had to find out how deeply in the hole we were and who exactly was attacking us. If my father couldn't figure out a way to save us, then I would.

"What's that look about?" Aryn signed quickly, worry growing on her face. "Georgia. What are you planning?"

I stalked over the door and gave her a wry grin, signing with my free hand. "Something unprincess-like."

Aryn's confusion covered her face but still she followed after me, not one to be left behind. It was one of the things I loved about her. No matter what mischief I got into she was right there by my side ready to get into it with me.

"Where are we going?" she signed haphazardly as we hurried down the hallway. "It's already dark. Most will be getting ready for bed now."

I shook my head. "Maybe my father but not Cal." I stopped us at a corner and grabbed her hand. "If they are hiding more from me, then now would be the time to hear it." I snorted and added on with a smirk, "you know what I mean."

We moved as quiet as mice through the corridors, making sure to stop and hide in the shadows when a guard or servant passed. While I didn't think they would tell on me, I didn't want to take the chance. I didn't want Cal to know I was coming. Or have a chance to hide anything he was keeping from me. Cal found my weakness, my people. I would not go another day without finding out his secret.

Cal's rooms were far enough away from my own that I could sleep soundly at night knowing there was a castle between us. However, it made it even harder to sneak around when I had to remember where every squeak and nook laid from before I lost my hearing. I waved a hand behind me to Aryn as we paused at the corner of the final corridor.

I wasn't surprised to find Cal's bedroom door partly open. No one else was using the guest wing and he'd probably thought he could treat it like his own home. After we were married it was going to be in any case. I swallowed down the bile that threatened to rise in my throat.

Aryn frowned in displeasure, hearing something I didn't. At the confusion on my face, she signed quietly, "Moans. And slapping flesh."

I took a moment to consider how that made me feel. While Cal and his brother had done all forms of atrocities on my person the one step they had thankfully not taken was forcing themselves onto me. So did it bother me to know that Cal was getting his pleasure from somewhere else when he was engaged to me? Fuck no. If only because it meant that he would not subject me to the same kind of experiences in our bedroom.

Pushing back the urge to run, I moved closer to the door. I placed my hand on the door frame, feeling the shaking their actions were causing to the walls around them. They must be very active indeed to cause such a disturbance. I only hoped the person was a willing participant and not someone Cal had bullied into his bed. Though, if so they were no friend of mine.

I pressed my face up against the door, peeking into the room through the crack no bigger than my two fingers. I could not see much, the bed just on the edge of my vision where I could see a sliver of a black haired woman's back, her body moving up and down in quick succession. Next to the bed sat a chair and I didn't have to guess who the person sitting in it was. I recognized that dark brown hair even from behind. The roll of the shoulders as Cal's brother, Lu, leaned forward and watched intently as the woman serviced Cal.

I could never quite figure out their relationship. It was disturbing to say the least. They shared everything. All their depravities. Their sick joy in pain that they bestowed on others.

Watching them now, I felt bad for whatever female allowed them to touch her voluntarily. You could not pay me a million gold to put myself in her position right now. However, since I haven't ended the engagement I could very well be in that position quite soon. I had to get something on them I could use.

The bed stopped moving, the woman shifted to the side and Cal threw his legs over the bed not bothering to cover up his nakedness. Though I despised my betrothed I took a moment to appreciate his muscular and defined form. If I didn't know the cruel and evil soul that laid beneath that god-like body I would understand the woman's eagerness to service him.

My eyes flicked to his lips which began to move, "We're done. Leave."

I only had a heartbeat to realize what was happening. Aryn grabbed my shoulder and pulled me back, shoving me against the wall and out of the doorframe. The door opened the rest of the way and a half-dressed woman scurried out, hurrying out the door and down the hallway so quickly she didn't notice Aryn and myself holding our breath as we pressed ourselves into the wall.

The door remained open. I didn't dare move closer to see around the corner for fear of being seen. Now that Cal's lust had been slackened, I didn't want to chance that his other needs had arisen.

The ground vibrated before growing closer. Aryn pulled me back further down the hallway as the door was pushed closed part way and then strangely it waved back and forth sending air and the distinct scent of sex into the hallway. I glanced back at Aryn with a questioning brow raised.

She rolled her eyes and signed, "Trying to get the smell of that slut out."

I gaped at her, responding, "That's not nice."

Aryn shook her head. "Their words, not mine." She peered over me toward the door where it had stopped at a slight ajar. "We should go." She tried to pull me away from the door.

I wiggled out of her grasp and moved back toward the door once more. I gestured vigorously behind me. "I can't leave until I have something to use. I won't live my life in fear of them."

Aryn patted my back encouragingly.

Controlling my breathing so as to not to draw their attention, I moved in close to the crack in the door. Now, Cal at least had pants on his chest still bare while he leaned against the bedpost. His sleaze of a brother had moved to the bed. I didn't want to think about what he was doing on that bed a few moments ago. The way he laid across it the sheet wrapped around him said more than I wanted to imagine. Lu's mouth moved and I focused on what he was saying rather than what he was doing.

"The troops are getting restless."

Cal glanced over his shoulder at his brother, turning his face away from the door while he spoke. Irritated at my lack of hearing, I tried to figure out what Cal was saying based on what his brother said.

Lu shrugged. "I'm not sure they will agree with you. You've been playing with her for too long. Just marry the chit and get it over with. Then we can move along with the plan."

My brows furrowed at the word, plan. What plan? What does marrying me have to do with it?

Cal still kept his back to the door, gesturing to his brother with an open hand. He was irritated by something. His shoulders were bunched and his neck tight. Though I couldn't see his mouth he was not happy with what his brother had said.

Lu sat up suddenly, the sheet in his hand as he narrowed his gaze on Cal. "You cannot be serious? At least, wait and see if the chit can produce an heir before killing her. And her father might have something to say about that."

Killing me! Cal planned on killing me? Why? Why bother with this farce of a betrothal if he only planned to kill me in the first place?

Ice slid into my veins and my hands shook. I didn't dare to look back at Aryn to see what she thought of their words. I had to find out the rest of their plan so I could stop them.

I missed Cal's response as Lu shook his head and leaned back onto the bed once more. "You are far more generous than I, brother. I would slaughter the lot of them and start anew with our own people. Enslaving them may be good for our coffers but not so much for morale. You'll have riots within the month."

Cal said something else, making his brother throw his head back and laugh. "What makes you think the drakes will do your dirty work for you? They hate us more than they hate the rest of the humans. I highly doubt their monster of a king will let you blame your culling on him."

The prince pulled his knife from his boot and slashed the air, mimicking a fight. I tried not to focus on the knife, the same knife that had cut into me not so long ago, and focus on what was being said.

"An excuse to get rid of the drakes or no, you have your hands full. I suggest you get started sooner rather than later." Lu's eyes gleamed and a small cruel smile curled his lips. "However, if you have no plans on fucking your betrothed then I would love a taste of her. Before you kill her, I mean."

A hand dragged me back into the hallway before I could see Cal's response. Aryn spun me around, her eyes wide and fearful and quickly signed for us to leave. I nodded in reply and hurried away from Cal's bedroom.

It wasn't until we arrived back at my room, the door slammed shut behind us that I realized I was shaking. Fear welled up in me, clogging my throat and other senses. I hadn't felt this helpless and vulnerable since my mother passed away. When I had my little sessions with Cal and Lu that came close, but nothing like this. I felt as if my very skin might vibrate off my body from how much I was shaking.

"Oh, Georgia," Aryn signed to me with tears in her eyes. "What are we going to do?"

I chewed on the end of my thumb, crossing one arm under the other to prop it up as I thought.

What were we going to do? I could go to my father and tell him what we found out. The problem being, would he believe me? Also, Cal could come up with some excuse saying I misunderstood them. Or move his plan up and kill my father and marry me anyway.

Then there was the fact that the people would still suffer. I was doing all of this for them. All the pain and scars the last few months had been for them. Now it seemed completely meaningless, if Cal was just going to kill them too. Or worse enslave them.

Fuck. What am I going to do?

My heart thudded rapidly in my chest as it all came down on me. What could I do? Nothing. I was just one person and not even a full one at that. I couldn't save myself let alone my kingdom. How am I going to figure this out without getting everyone dead in the process?

Aryn gestured to me. "Can you believe the gall of that bastard to blame his actions on the drakes? They have enough of a bad reputation without being that ass's patsy. Why, if I was the drakes, I would fry his ass and put him on a pike."

My heart stopped. The drakes!

That was it. That was how I was going to save my kingdom. A smile curled up my face and I let out a laugh, grabbing Aryn's hands with mine.

Aryn gave me a strange look before releasing my hand to cup my face. "Are you okay? I know this is a lot of information but we will figure this out. I won't let them hurt you. I promise."

I shook my head and grinned down at her. Gesturing quickly, I said, "Don't you see? That's the answer to our problem."

"What is?" Aryn signed back.

"The drakes."

Chapter 3

THE COOL NIGHT AIR PUSHED against me, finding every place my cloak did not cover. Why did I think this was a good idea again? Oh, right. It was better than what awaited me at home. The handsome face of my betrothed flashed through my face and I forced the bile down before it surfaced.

Shivering, I focused on the trees of the forest around us rather than the biting cold. Normally this time of year the air would be crisp but for some reason the gods deemed to test me by making the night I chose to run away to be the one night the temperature would drop. I could even see my breath before me and the frost on the leaves of the trees.

Aryn waved a hand at me, drawing my attention from the trees. "Are you sure this is a good idea?" Her face was pinched with worry and she shifted so much on her horse that the poor beast shook its head with annoyance.

I patted my own mare to reassure her that everything was alright as I signed, "Yes, Aryn for the last time. I'm sure. There's no other way. We have to stop the marriage."

Aryn pulled her lower lip between her teeth and worried it so hard I worried she'd bite through the thing. "But what can the drakes do? They're just as bad as Cal if not worse. Aren't you worried they will kill you on sight?"

I snorted, adjusting my skirts around my legs to keep out the cold. "I have to try. I can't just sit by and do nothing. Then my life and my people's lives would be forfeit all for those smarmy brothers."

Aryn shoulders bunched up and dropped in a huff as she signed quickly in the pale moon light. "Maybe you should just tell your father? He could figure this out. It shouldn't be on your shoulders."

I tugged on my reins to slow up my mare so I could sign back. "Suppose he believes me? What would he do? We have no money, our army is nothing compared to Cal's. We need help, Aryn."

"And you think you can convince the drakes to help?"

I didn't answer her. I didn't know. I could only hold my breath and pray to whatever gods were listening that I was doing the right thing and they would help me through it.

"Georgia," Aryn brought her horse to a stop, her hand outstretched to me. "Are you alright?"

I repressed a shudder, brushing my face against the side of my cloak. No. I wasn't. I couldn't tell her that though then she'd prod further into what Cal and his nasty brother had done to me. Aryn had seen the scars. Had cared for the wounds but she didn't know how deep it went and how far into my very being they had ingrained themselves. I had to destroy them, the way they tried to destroy me.

"This has to work." My hands stung from the cold and I wished I'd had the forethought to bring my gloves with me. I signed quicker so I could bury my hands into my cloak once more. "The drakes will think I'm a helpless princess taking a night ride and think they have found themselves something rewarding. With any luck they take me to their king and I can plead our case."

Aryn shook her head, her auburn hair coming out from beneath her hood. "I don't think anyone has ever called you helpless. And you are putting a lot of faith into this plan. What if the drakes don't believe you? What if this is a big mistake?" Aryn gripped her throat with a horrified expression. "What if they choose to send back your head as a message instead?"

Patience wearing thin, I pulled my horse to a stand still and turned to Aryn. "And what if the sky falls down and kills us all? Really Aryn, if you don't take any chances how can you say you've really lived?"

"I take chances." Aryn pointed her nose in the air. "I'm taking a chance right now coming with you when I could be curled up in my bed right now instead of freezing my bottom off making sure you don't get yourself killed."

I rolled my eyes. "No one said you had to come. Like you said, I can take care of myself."

"And yet," Aryn jumped in waving a hand in my direction. "Here you are in the middle of Grebe Forest with no provisions and in nothing but your night dress. You should have taken more time to think this through."

My lips turned down at the sides. "And give Cal time to move forward with his plan?"

"You don't know that. He wasn't going to do anything until you got married. You had time."

"No, I didn't. Also, if I had changed or brought provisions then it would look a bit odd when they caught me, wouldn't it? Like I was purposely running away rather than being reckless?" The last thing I needed was to be killed on sight or worse sent back to the palace. I had to get the drake king to listen to me. For more than just my sake.

Aryn closed her eyes for a moment taking a deep breath in and then out before she turned back to me. "Fine. Let's just get this over with."

I grinned broadly. "That's more like it!" I signed to her before flicking my reins and calling out, "hiyah!" My horse shot through the forest at a galloping sprint. The wind blew through my midnight black hair. I closed my eyes and let myself fall into the feeling. The feeling of being free.

Ever since my father had announced my engagement to Cal it felt as if a noose had gone around my neck. Then every day since, the noose grew tighter and tighter until I couldn't scream, I couldn't breath, I was suffocating under the pending nuptials and Cal's cruel treatment of me.

Along with what I had overhead, today was the final knot in my noose.

Usually Cal did not go so far as to cut me up. However, with his brother Lu there to egg him on, Cal had taken delight into carving my skin up, marking me permanently with his touch. I could still feel his breath on my face as he hovered over my body, seeing his mouth move through the tears burning in my eyes.

"Now everyone will know you are mine," Cal murmured as he carved his name into my skin while his brother held me down, his sweaty hand over my mouth so I couldn't scream.

My hand released the rein and reached up to touch my side. I stopped myself before I made contact, pushing back the angry tears. I would not be defined by my scars. I was stronger than that and I would prove it to Cal, Lu, and my father. Once and for all.

"How much further do you think?" Aryn questioned as we came to the edge of Grebe forest. So far we hadn't encountered anyone. Especially, not the drake guards we'd been warned that supposedly frequented the forest.

My brows furrowed as I searched the area, my hands tightening on the reins as I slowed us down to a trot so I could sign. "We should have found someone by now. Do you think we should go further? Or walk the length of the forest again?"

I twisted in my saddle to look at her.

Aryn sat on her horse as still as a statue, the sharp edge of a long spear at her throat held by a large cloaked figure. Eyes wide, she tried to say something to me with her eyes. I tried to figure out what she was trying to tell me before a sharp pain sprang up in the back of my head and then everything went dark.

A vicious jostling awoke me. It took me a moment to figure out where I was. My face pressed against the side of my horse, and the ground above my head. I shifted and tried to move my hands. I couldn't. Hands and feet bound, I found myself thrown over the side of my horse. A sharp smack to my back made me stop moving. I blinked into the dim light and twisted my head sideways, searching for the face of my captor.

They say the drakes were descended from dragons. A once proud race that flew across the world claiming land and riches for their own. Then they met humans. The humans hunted them to the ends of the world, killing their young, stealing their horde, until the few dragons that were left were desperate to survive.

Calling on their magics, they took the form of humans and gave up their love for the sky so they could blend in and no longer be hunted. Which would have worked well had they not decided to go one step further and not only live as humans but mate with them as well. The result of those couplings was a surprise to all, especially the human parts. For though the dragons could hide their true selves with magic, they could not change the basic parts of them and so those parts came out in other ways.

Their children.

I'd never seen a drake. Never had the urge to seek them out. There were books though. Books that depicted multi-hued skin covered in scales, horns protruding from their heads, and tails so long and thick that they could be used as a mighty weapon against their enemies.

The creatures holding me captive were all those things and more. While yes, he, I assumed it was a he for the lack of breasts where his muscular chest was exposed, had an odd brown green coloring, more along the lines of a reptile than any human being, he also had a humanoid face. His jawline and nose were just as a human male's would be, straight and protruding with two openings in the nostrils. His mouth which replaced what I would have thought would be a muzzle, ready to clamp down on unsuspecting prey.

The first hint of anything inhuman on his face was the eyes. Golden orbs with a slit pupil focused straight ahead unaware of my staring. My gaze slid over the horns that came out of his head on either side and the dark brown hair that covered his scalp, falling along the side of his face and fastening into a braid.

Metal and stone plates lined his arms and upper body, leaving his chest to waist bare. A thick muscular thigh sat inches from my face bare except for the braces on his knee and shins, boots hid his feet from me leaving me to wonder if they were clawed like their ancestors.

My pulse raced and my mind whirled as I tried to think of a way out of this situation. I almost laughed out loud but caught myself.

This had been the plan after all. Wander the woods until the drakes find me, get captured, be demanded to be brought before their king, and then beg him to help save both our people. Now, here I was slung over my own horse wanting nothing more than a way from this.

What the hell was I thinking? I couldn't do this. These were obviously hard worn warriors who would likely kill me as soon as they got me back to their camp. Why would they listen to me? A princess and a nearly broken one at that.

No. Get it together, Georgia. You will not let Cal take the last part of you away. You are stronger than that. Stronger than this. Besides, what's so scary about this drake? He's handsome in an unhuman way, if one could overlook my flaws there was no reason I wouldn't be able to do the same.

A large thick object swung out from behind the drake and spikes came dangerously close to my face. A sound escaped my throat drawing the attention of my captor.

I stilled and drew away from what I now saw was his tail. At least that bit was true.

The drake poked at me and his lips moved, "Quiet female, or you will spook the horse."

For a moment I contemplated not answering him. I had never seen my disability as a weakness. Never needed to. In the palace, everyone bent over backward to learn how to communicate with me and tried their best to make me feel normal. It wasn't until Cal showed up

45

that I felt anything other than that. And now facing a new obstacle, I realized I wasn't so sure them knowing about my disadvantage was a good thing.

I'd have to fake it. Pretend that I knew what they were saying by reading their lips and body language. I just hoped that I didn't get found out before I got what I wanted.

"Where are we going?" The words felt foreign on my tongue. I tried not to speak often, I'd been told by many that my voice had lost its once lovely lilt to it and now seemed as if I were talking through a filter of water.

I had to push the feeling of discomfort away. With people like Cal now in my life, I needed to get over it. I didn't want it used against me the way he did. I wouldn't be at the mercy of anyone again.

The drake threw his head back, his laughter shaking the horse beneath me. He turned his head toward something behind me and I could barely make out his lips moving. "'Where are we going,' she asks? The female is too stupid to be scared."

I assumed there was another drake on Aryn's horse with my handmaiden thrown over the way I had been so graciously done. I wished I was turned the other way so at least I could see her and make sure that she is alright.

"Where's my friend?" I tried again, clearing my throat. "I am not a sack of potatoes."

The drake smacked me on the backside and laughed again. This time speaking directly to me rather than his friend. "You should worry more about yourself than your friend. When we get to the Clan you will see why the drakes are feared. We do not take trespassers in our woods lightly."

It was on the tip of my tongue to argue back that this was not their woods, it belonged to my father. I didn't think it was wise to let them know who I was right away. I wanted to see the king and if I let this lowly drake know what a prized possession he had in his hands then he might choose to use me on his own then I would be back where I started. At the mercy of Cal.

The horses continued for so long that I eventually dozed off. I didn't know how I could sleep at a time like this. My position wasn't the most comfortable. Perhaps it was exhaustion from all the excitement and horror of the day. Cal's latest abuse, finding out about my impending death, and now being captured by the drakes. It was bound to catch up to me eventually.

I didn't know how long it was before I woke with a start. The horse had come to a stop. My captor's seat was no longer filled and yet I was still bound and on the horse. Searching the area before me, all I could see was hay and dirt covered ground. I tried to twist around in the saddle to see further into the covered area that I was beginning to suspect was a stable and shifted just a bit too much. My body careened over the side, head first for the ground. I put my bound hands over my face. I landed with a hard bounce.

Groaning, I laid on my side for a moment, trying to catch the breath that had been knocked out of me. When no one came running at my fall, I took the time to wiggle around on the ground until I was sitting up on my knees. Huffing at the exertion, I cursed the drake for binding my hands and feet. Where did he think I was going to go? They caught us easily enough, they could do it again.

Scanning my surroundings, I saw that it was indeed a stable. Several other horses sat in their stalls, happy as can be though they were in the camp of monsters. I didn't see any drakes around or Aryn. Using my feet to scooch myself to turn in place, I peered under my horse searching for Aryn's horse. When I saw the horse, I almost crawled under mine just to get to it but quickly made myself worm around her to get to the other side, my dress had to be ruined by now from all the crawling in the dirt and hay but I didn't care. I only wanted to be sure Aryn was alright.

Aryn's mop of red hair hung over the side of her horse, not moving. Panic set in. I pushed myself to my knees, and shook her shoulder, saying her name aloud, "Aryn. Aryn. Wake up."

She moved slightly and turned her face toward me, breathing heavily in my face. I grimaced. Shoving her with my bound hands, I scowled. Wake up, already. We had to figure out what we were going to do before the drakes got back. Aryn simply shifted and continued to sleep.

Fuck. I sank back to my knees and glanced around the stable. There had to be something I could use...ah! I crawled across the ground on my knees until I came to an ax. My eyes darted around the room continuously searching for anyone coming while I sawed away at the bindings on my hands. With a breath of relief, I broke the ropes and then worked on the ones on my legs. Once I was free, I hurried over to Aryn.

This time I did not try to gently wake her. I slapped Aryn across the face so hard that she jolted and jerked in place, falling off the horse in the same manner I had. I tried to grab her to soften her fall but it didn't work out very well. Aryn landed hard and I rushed to her side. Gesturing, I'm sorry over and over again.

Aryn sat up awkwardly, her eyes darting from side to side. When they landed on me, she grabbed at me only to notice she was bound. I held up my hand for her to hold on and went to grab the ax. Rushing back to her side, I worked on her bindings as quickly as possible without hurting her. Her hands finally free, Aryn signed frantically, "Where are we?"

I shook my head and paused to sign back. "Stables."

"What's going on? Where are the drakes?" Her hand movements were so fast and sloppy that I had a hard time understanding her.

Grabbing her hands, I locked my eyes with her and said, "We have to get out of here."

Her mouth moved slowly so I could understand. "What about the king? The plan?"

I dropped my eyes and pulled her to her feet before signing, "Forget about it. We'll find another way. This was a rash and impulsive idea. There's no way they will believe us. I hardly believe us."

Moving to my horse, Aryn grabbed me and jerked me back around. "You will not give up. You can do this. It is a good plan. If anyone can convince the drake king to help, it is you." She gestured at my body with a sad look. "You have the scars to prove it."

I tried not to flinch at her words. She was right. I was strong enough to do this. I had to do this. For my people. For my father. And most importantly for me.

Chapter 4

"SOMEONE IS COMING," ARYN told me and grabbed me by the shoulders. "What do we do?"

Instead of signing, I said out loud in a hurried whisper, "Do not sign. Don't let them know I can't hear. Try to angle yourself so I can read your lips if need be."

"Won't they suspect something?" She mouthed instead of signing.

I shook my head. "Say you speak for me or something. Make them think I'm some prissy princess who can't be bothered to respond back to those who aren't worth her time."

Before Aryn could say anything else to me, her gaze shot behind me. "Get away from us." She shoved me behind her and shifted so that I could see her face. "I demand that you let us leave right now. Don't you know who we are?"

The drake that had been on my horse entered with another one of the same physical traits except his skin or scales — I couldn't tell which was more prominent — were more of a deep red. He had the same yellow slit eyes as the first one and he too wore armor that kept his chest bare and only a loin cloth covered his genitals. At least, I assumed they had them. Did dragons have cocks? They laid eggs, didn't they? I wasn't sure and at the moment, all my lessons were scrambled in my brain while I tried to manage the situation at hand.

"You will see the king and you can tell him all about who you are," the drake laughed and stalked toward us.

Aryn pushed back against me, trying to put herself between me and the drake. I wasn't about to have that. I grabbed the ax and bared my teeth at him, daring the drake to come get us.

The drake took one look at me and my ax and smirked. Before I could move my arms to swing, he grabbed the ax out of my hands and threw it across the room where it stuck in the stone of the wall. Eyes wide, my heart ratchet up a notch and I asked myself again why I thought this was a good idea.

Large hands with sharp claws wrapped around the back of my neck, jerking me forward until I was a hair's breadth from the drake. I tried to read his lips as he spoke, his breath against my face but my eyes kept locking on those slitted eyes and the large horns protruding from his head and I completely missed what he said.

When I didn't respond, the drake sneered and shoved me forward. Aryn hurried after me, clasping onto my arm. Her fingers tightened on my arm and I winced. I whispered to her, "What did he say?"

Aryn shook her head and mouthed, "Just threatening you." She paused for a moment, her mouth pinching together. "He thinks you are dumb in the head."

I bobbed my head and muttered, "Good."

I wanted them to underestimate me. People had underestimated me my whole life and once I lost my hearing it was even worse. I have learned to use that to my advantage. You could get away with all kinds of things when they don't expect it to come from you.

The drake shoved at my back and I stumbled, glaring over my shoulder at him.

He scowled and his lips formed the word, "Move."

Resisting the urge to shoot him a rude gesture, I continued to play the dumb princess with not enough sense to stay alive. Though sadly I was beginning to think that wasn't much further from the truth.

We were ushered down a long hallway of stone and it took me a few moments to realize we had to be underneath Mount Boyon. There was no other mountain close to the forest and no one had ever been able to figure out where the drakes lived and now I knew. Which only made my stomach sink further. They would not bring us here unless they didn't intend for us to ever leave.

I squeezed Aryn's hand tightly and swallowed. I could do this. I had to do this. For myself and my people. I had faced worse. I could face the drakes.

I lost track of how many turns we took, my heart thudding so hard against my chest it was hard to pay attention to anything else.

We passed drakes on the way through, each of them ranging in different colors and sizes. I had yet to see one that could be considered female and I wasn't sure if that was a good thing or a bad one. Either way, I couldn't remove this feeling of dread from my throat. It sat there clogging my breath so that they came out in hard forced pants.

Aryn slid a hand around my shoulders and rubbed her palm up and down my back.

Looking at her, I realized I had to get it together. Aryn had come here for me. I couldn't be the one who broke apart now. Forcing a weak smile, I inhaled deeply telling myself to just breathe. I just had to convince the king of the drakes that it would be beneficial for him to help me. That's all. It wasn't that hard. We both needed something. Why not help each other out? Yes, that was it. I could do this.

We entered a large chamber filled with drakes on either side of a walkway. All eyes turned to us. My feet slowed beneath me and the drake behind me pushed me forward, making me stumble and half fall to the ground. Aryn caught me by the arm she was holding, keeping me from completely collapsing on the ground. I glared down at the dirt floor, my palms burning from impact.

Slowly, I lifted my head and saw the jeering faces of the drakes. They pointed and grabbed at their genitals, making it quite clear what they wanted to do to us. Swallowing down the bile in my throat, I climbed back to my feet.

Aryn gripped my arm and mouthed if I was alright.

I nodded and proceeded forward. My eyes locked onto the front of the chamber. A large stone and bone structure sat at the front of the room and it took me a moment to realize that it was a throne.

This must be where the drake king lorded over his people.

The throne was empty right now but I had no doubt that it wouldn't be for long.

The drake leading us grabbed me by the shoulder once we arrived at the front of the room where the drakes had kept a good distance from the throne as if they too feared it. The drake's hand on my shoulder pushed down and I sneered over my shoulder at him.

"Kneel," his lips commanded.

"I will not." I spat back. I would not lower myself to a monster I had not even met yet. By the gods I was a princess, not some lowly peon.

When I didn't move, the drake kicked the back of my knee, causing it to buckle and I fell to my knees hard enough that my teeth jarred in my head. Aryn lowered to her knees without being forced and in hindsight I probably should have waited to use my voice for something more important than kneeling. They didn't know who I was or what I wanted, just that they had found me in their woods. I was a trespasser and in most kingdoms that was punishable by death. I was lucky to still be alive.

We waited on our knees for what felt like hours. My eyes scanned the room, searching for any sign of this supposed drake king. The other drakes talked amongst themselves, every once in a while glancing our way and giving vulgar gestures. Some didn't even bother to keep their thoughts in their heads, their mouths moving as they licked their sharp fangs with their long split tongue, saying everything they wanted to do to us.

A shudder ran through me and I forced my face forward, unable to bear seeing anymore.

After a few moments, the air stilled and everyone turned to the front. Tremors rattled the ground beneath my knees and my gaze jerked to the open stone entry to the left of the throne at the backside of the room. Two drakes came out of the entrance first, both of them a golden yellow with dark red hair. They wore matching colored gray and white armor, though one carried a curved sword and the other a long two sided battle ax that crossed over the length of his back. Their tails swished from one side to the other as they entered, almost as menacing as they were with a spiked ring looping around the end of them.

The two drakes stopped on either side of the throne, their eyes, a liquid golden green, scanned the crowd before falling onto Aryn and me. Curiosity filled the eyes of one while distrust in the other. I paid their looks no mind, they didn't matter anyway. Only the drake king. He was who I had to win over.

I didn't have long to wait now, for the drake king prowled through the doorway seconds later. Larger than most of the drakes we had encountered so far, his skin was the same golden hue as the first two drakes except his hair was a brighter colored red which he wore shaved on the sides and long on top, poofing up between the two off white horns on his head. Each horn had a metal ring wrapped around the base of it that matched the same one that he had on the end of his tail. The other drakes did not have this accessory, only the king and the two drakes before us. Did it have a special meaning?

The drake king held no weapon. He didn't need it. His mere presence was enough of a threat. He kept his chest bare with leather straps criss crossing over it to hold the metal and stone plates on his shoulders. Bracers decorated each of his forearms and shins as well as plates on his knees. Did he wear them all the time? It couldn't be comfortable. And here I thought corsets were the worst thing I could be forced to wear.

Against my better judgment, my eyes moved along the length of the drake king's body, taking in the muscular thighs barely hidden by the burlap colored cloth covering his genitals. He had muscles in every place you could see and that was pretty much everywhere. I swallowed the thump that had formed in my throat. This was not a creature to trifle with and here I was trying to trick him into helping me.

My gaze slid up the drake king's body and locked with his eyes. Those yellow green slitted eyes narrowed on me, his thin mouth twisting to the side with displeasure. He slid into his throne, his tail sliding to one side to accommodate him. Then his mouth moved.

"What is this?"

I couldn't see the drake behind me so it was impossible to tell what he said in return but I could guess. He was likely

60

telling him what had happened and where he had found us.

The drake king turned his attention back to Aryn and me. "What were you doing in Grebe Forest?"

I let Aryn answer for me, better to start making them believe the lie we were selling now. I watched her out of the corner of my eyes as she responded to the drake king.

"We were taking a nightly ride, is that a crime amongst you beast?"

My lips twitched at her words. I forced it down, making my face into the penchant of boredom.

The drake king glanced from Aryn to me and leaned forward in his throne, his elbows on his knees. "And do you regularly ride in your nightgowns?"

I could feel the eyes of the drakes on my skin, the thin material of my nightgown clung to me from sweat and fear. I had no doubt it did little to hide my body from their leering eyes.

Aryn shrugged next to me. "My charge does what she likes."

"And does your charge not speak?" The way his eyes focused on me as his mouth moved was almost enough for me to break character and stand up for myself but I held back.

"When someone is worth speaking to."

I could almost feel the air suck out of the room from the startled looks on the drakes' faces around the room. Once more I had to tamper down my urge to smile. Apparently, no one dared speak to their king in such a manner. However, I was beyond letting pompous assholes walk all over me. It was my turn to fight back.

To my surprise, the drake king didn't lash out at Aryn's words. He skimmed over the two of us, his face was harder to read than others. Most people had a hard time keeping their thoughts off their face. Not him. He could very well be contemplating his next meal as planning our deaths for all I could tell.

His next words though, caused a surprised gasp from me.

"What would you give me to spare your lives?" His clawed finger skimmed over his lip, his gaze focusing on me and not Aryn. It seemed he had already decided what he wanted and simply wanted us to offer it to him.

"Why would we offer you anything?" Aryn retorted very much playing the warrior though I knew for a fact she was close to wetting herself. No one could bullshit as well as Aryn could, I'd learned from the best after all. "It was a simple misunderstanding. Return us to which you found us and we will keep our silence."

The drake king stared at her for a long moment before sliding those beryl colored eyes toward me. Our gazes locked and I couldn't pull away. It was as if something were prickling at my head, trying to get inside. A kind of warmth spread over my body and I licked my lips, his eyes dipped down to that movement.

Aryn squeezed my hand, breaking whatever spell held me in the drake king's gaze. "Well? Will you leave us to return home with none the wiser and no blood to be shed?"

The drake king answered with his eyes never leaving my face. "No."

Before Aryn could answer, I turned to her, placing my face near her ear so that no one else could hear. I barely opened my mouth as I spoke into her ears, hoping my voice was low enough not to be heard. The words I said caused Aryn to still, her back going rigid and her eyes wide. She stared at me as I moved away from her. "Are you sure?" her eyes said even though her mouth did not move.

I bobbed my head once, before turning my attention back to the drake king.

I didn't watch Aryn as she portrayed my words. I kept my gaze on the drake king.

How would he react when Aryn offered me to him? Would he be delighted? Disgusted? Neutral? I found myself wanting to cause a rise out of this otherwise unyielding creature.

To my utter disappointment, the drake king did not react more than the slight narrowing of his eyes. "Very well." He stood from his throne and stalked out of the room.

The other two drakes near the throne moved toward us. I angled away from them as the first one grabbed me by the arm and jerked me to my feet. The other one grabbed Aryn in the same manner and led her back toward the way we came.

I twisted in the drake's hands, trying to see where they were taking her. Aryn's eyes filled with panic and her mouth moved quickly, "Don't...stay...." I frowned at her words. What was she trying to say?

I wasn't able to stand there and contemplate them. The drake holding onto me began to pull me toward the direction the drake king had gone. I didn't fight him. There was no point. I'd offered myself to the drake king and now I had to follow through with it.

The drake leading me squeezed my arm and stopped in the narrow hallway. It was then I realized he had said something to me. I watched his face as his mouth moved again. One of his eyes focused on me while the other stared at nothing, the coloring a milky yellow, a set of claw marks scored across his eye, starting at the hairline and ending at the edge of his perfectly shaped bow lips.

"Don't make him angry."

I snorted.

This made the drake's brows shoot up in surprise. "You are either brave or extremely stupid."

I scowled at him.

The drake smirked. "I'm betting on stupid." Before pushing me toward an open doorway and into the drake king's bedroom.

Chapter 5

WHAT WAS WITH ALL THE pushing? I barely kept myself from falling on my face as I caught myself on the side table just inside the door.

I spun around to let the drake know exactly how I felt about his manhandling only to find the door closing in my face. The drake left me without telling me what to do or where to go. Or even where the drake king was.

Turning back to the bedroom, I sighed. Well this was just great. What did I do now?

Scanning the room, I was pleasantly surprised to see that at least the drake king lived like a civilized person and not some animal rolling around in filth on the ground. I walked across the dirt floor pausing to bend down and touch the soft fur of the animal skin spread out across the middle of the room. I suppose it was better than a dirty cell. Though, I had expected the drake king to be waiting, ready to make good on my offer.

My eyes darted to the bed and I licked my lips.

What would it be like? Would the drake king be rough or did he only want a release? I could do that. I'd been told on more than one occasion that I knew exactly how fast and firm to service a cock to completion. I wouldn't say that it was due to my need to be more attentive outside of hearing my partner's pleasure, but it certainly didn't hurt.

A part of me was a bit relieved to know he wasn't here ready to mount me like some animal. I hadn't been thinking clearly about it when I had offered myself up to the drake king. I wish I could say that I had only been thinking about my people's survival and getting Aryn out of there alive. That hadn't been the case. While this had been the plan all along, to gain the drake king's trust so that he would help me, at that moment all I could think about was the warmth that had spread through my body. One that I knew...I knew from just those eyes piercing into me could be even better.

However, I certainly didn't want Aryn to suffer for my rash decisions. If anyone was going to pay the price to save our people then it would be me. I'd already given enough to Cal and Lu, this time I wanted it to be my choice.

I contemplated waiting for the drake king on his bed naked. That would certainly make a statement. It would put me in charge of the situation opposed to waiting around for the drake king to show himself and decide he wanted to fuck me.

A small vibration underneath my feet announced his presence. Even if I hadn't felt the shift in the air, the very feel of the drake king in the room was enough to let me know. The room became smaller and the air became thicker with a smoky scent that reminded me of the woods and rain storms. My mouth grew dry as I slowly shifted around to face the drake king.

My body stiffened under his scrutinizing gaze. While he took his time looking me over once more, there was still that same suspicious glint in his eyes. One that said he didn't trust me regardless of my attempts to look and seem like a feeble human woman. He didn't believe me for one second.

I lifted my chin in challenge. I'd just have to try harder to get him to trust me.

"You've offered yourself to me and yet you stand here still clothed." He gestured toward me with a scowl. "Does the word of Kinokos mean so little that it is so easily forgotten?"

The drake king stalked into the room and breezed past me, barely giving me a second glance as he unclipped the left shoulder plate and let it slide down his muscular arm, the burnt yellow-orange of his skin an astute contrast to the silver and white of his armor. The plate dropped to the ground and bounced once toward me.

To my disappointment, I jerked back from it like it was a snake about to bite me. What was wrong with me? It was just a piece of armor. He hadn't even done anything to warrant my fear yet. At this rate, I'd never even get to the seduction part.

My eyes followed his large, calloused hands as they unfastened the other shoulder plate. This time he didn't let it drop to the floor but held it in his hand. My gaze lifted to the face of my new master, those liquid yellow-green eyes locked on me with indifference. "Well? Are you a liar as well as a coward?"

My eyes trained on his lips as he formed the words, each movement making my blood boil. I shoved my long dark braid over my shoulder and glowered.

Keeping my eyes locked onto those slitted eyes, I gripped the neckline of my night dress and pulled it down my shoulder none too gently before the other followed. Untying the bodice without removing my gaze from the drake king's face, I started to drop the material, my heart pounding so hard in my chest it hurt.

No one but Aryn had seen me without my clothing on since my private time with my betrothed. Aryn had even dismissed my usual maids to keep them from seeing my shame. To be standing here in front of the drake king about to show this intimate part of myself...I think I was going to be sick.

The drake king stared at me, his lips pursed tightly and jaw tightened. Then his lips moved in a distinctive word. "Stop."

My hands froze. I almost let out a breath showing him my relief to stop. I shouldn't be relieved. This was my idea. I couldn't very well go through with my plan if I couldn't bring myself to get naked in front of the drake king.

His lips moved again. This time so minutely I couldn't tell what he said. I squinted at his lips trying to decipher his words. Then they stopped moving and the sharp angles of his face grew even sharper as his brows furrowed together.

I shook my head. Unable to figure out what he had said and unwilling to give myself away just yet.

Then the Drake king surprised me yet again.

You cannot hear, can you?

I jumped back from him, my eyes blinking rapidly at what I'd just heard. But his lips did not move even when he spoke in my head once more. *Forgive me for not realizing sooner.*

My eyes narrowed on the beast trying to figure out if this was some trick to set me off balance. The drake king cocked his head to the side and reached out to touch the side of my face. When I flinched he dropped his hand.

It is not a trick. I'm inside your head. What I wish to know is why did your companion not say you were unable to hear before?

Scowling, I grabbed the shoulders of my dress and pulled it back into place. Having someone in my head was much worse when I was half clothed.

It seems I have been a dim-witted king to not have realized your needs sooner.

I watched him with wary eyes. Unsure of what to do or even what to think at that moment. Could he hear everything in my head?

His lips curled up in a smile that made my stomach flip. *Not everything. Only those thoughts you project loudly like you are now.*

Suddenly, it seemed as if a whole new door had opened to me. I knew the drakes had powers that we humans had never even dreamed of but mind reading? What else could they do?

His face lit up at my questions and he laughed. It shook his whole body and it made me want to touch his chest to see if it was as full bodied as it seemed.

When he was finished, the drake king offered me his hand. *Let us begin anew. I am Ryu.*

I stared down at his hand before cautiously sliding my smaller one into it. His hand was rough but not unpleasantly so and strong as he gripped my hand in his. The thought of what those hands could do to me sent a shudder through me though I wasn't quite sure if it was good or bad.

What is your name, pet?

My lips formed a stern line at the nickname as I tightened my hand on his in return. He thought me completely harmless now that he knew about my disability and instead of being happy about being able to use it against him, rage filled my chest.

"I am Princess Georgia of the Kinokos kingdom," I snarled, leveling a glare on the drake king as I jerked my hand out of his grasp. "And I am no one's pet."

Ryu's brows rose, surprise covering his face. "So you can speak. I wondered." This he said aloud, his lips moving precisely so that I could read them. *Or do you simply pretend to not know what I am saying?*

My lips pinched together and I leaned away from the drake king. *Get out of my head!*

Sitting down on the edge of his bed, Ryu proceeded to remove the bracers on his arms and then the greaves on either shin. Next came his elbow and knee guards, then his hands went to the cloth at his waist and I felt the sound escape my throat before I could help it.

Ryu paused, arching a brow at me.

Swallowing, I said aloud, "What are you doing?" I hadn't used my voice this much in a long time, it felt odd after so long of using my hands. I had to clutch my dress tighter in my hands to keep myself from using the signs I would normally use as I spoke.

That long forked tongue slid out of his mouth and swept along the edges of his mouth before slithering back in as he smirked. "It's late. I do not know about human females but I am exhausted and I'm getting ready for bed."

I gaped at him. I couldn't even voice my confusion.

This monster was just going to get ready for bed and let me stand here like a fool waiting for him to bed me? I squeezed my eyes shut and tried not to think about it.

I do not bed unwilling women.

This wouldn't do at all. I couldn't wrap him around my finger if he wouldn't bed me. I thought I had a handle on my fear but it seems that I needed to practice more. Straightening my back, I stepped up to the bed where he sat and lowered to my knees.

What are you doing?

I blinked up at him with a determined look on my face. *What was agreed upon.*

Not moving away from me, I could feel Ryu's eyes on me as I reached for the cloth covering his cock.

I breathed in and held it as my hands lifted the cloth and exposed what was beneath. The muscle in his thigh twitched at my touch, my hand so much smaller in comparison to the massive length hidden beneath the material.

I swallowed down the ball in my throat, my eyes blinking up to meet his gaze while my hand curled around him. Those slitted eyes watched me almost daring me to keep going.

Exploring the length of him, I surveyed what I was working with. Unlike the scales that decorated the rest of his body, his cock was smooth and hard as steel beneath the pale golden flesh.

I stroked my hand up and down his length for a moment, getting the feel of him. I cupped the sacks of flesh beneath his cock, finding them not unlike those of a human though these had sprinkles of scales on them unlike his length.

Ryu lifted his hands and I thought for a moment that he might push me away but paused, flexing the fingers before laying them on the top of his thighs. It seemed that he would be letting me take the lead on this. Good. Let's see how scary the drake king was when a little human woman makes him come apart in her mouth.

As if anticipating what I was about to do, the drake king's hand found the length of my braid. He wrapped it around his hand and tugged me forward so that his cock bumped against my chin and lips.

Licking my lips, I flicked the muscle out to taste the tip of him. Salty but earthy, much better than some of the men I'd been with before. Unable to hold back my curiosity any longer, I wrapped my lips around the head of him, dipping my head down until I had as much of him as I could in my mouth. Though I was able to take a lot there was still quite a bit left over for my hands to hold onto. I'd never had someone this size before. Hardly any of the men back at court were so well endowed.

He tugged on my braid, pulling my eyes up.

Stop thinking of other males with my cock in your mouth.

Males were all the same.

Resisting the urge to roll my eyes, I swallowed against the head of his cock, making that claw holding my hair tighten more.

I shifted on my knees to a more comfortable position while I rocked myself back and forth, bobbing my head up and down over his cock. I tried to take as much of him in as possible, making my eyes water and the ability to breath near impossible. Ryu didn't force me to take more, he simply held his hand there in my hair, not controlling but ready to take charge at any moment. The very thought made my center heat up and I ached for my own release.

Ignoring my own needs, I pushed ahead, moving more quickly finding a rhythm that made his whole body vibrate. It got so violent at one point that my eyes flicked up to make sure I hadn't done anything wrong, only to see Ryu's bare chest burning red beneath the flesh and scales. Curiosity and worry had me pulling away. Clawed hands grasped either side of my head, shoving my mouth back down on his length. My gaze locked with Ryu's and I knew he was close seconds before hot thick streams of it coated the inside of my mouth and throat. There was so much of it that it dribbled out of my mouth. The whole experience made me want to climb into his lap and ride him until I found oblivion.

I couldn't. This wasn't about my pleasure. This was about him and making him want me so badly that he would do anything for me. Even take down a whole kingdom.

When the last of his release filled me, Ryu released my head and I drew back with a hard swallow and gasp. I swiped the remnants of him off my face with my fingers, making sure to lick them clean where he could see it, a moan coming from my chest.

You should not have done that.

My eyes flew open at the words in my head, anger and confusion building inside of me.

Done what?

Ryu ignored my question or didn't hear it as he stood from the bed and moved over to the torches hanging from the walls. One by one he put them out with what looked like the back of a turtle shell until he was down to one. Then he turned to me. *Get in the bed.*

Confused by his words after he just said he didn't want to bed me, I hesitated.

Seeing my hesitation, Ryu held the turtle shell over the torch, his words echoing in my head. *Suit yourself. It will be pitch black in here when I put this light out and I do not think humans can see in the dark.*

When his hand inched forward, I jumped to do what he had told me. Once I was seated, the drake king put the light out and we were indeed in complete darkness. I sat on the edge of the bed as stiff as a board, wondering what he would do next.

Since I couldn't see him or hear him except the occasional small vibration as he moved across the floor, I was left completely to his devices. Panic rose up in my throat, the image of hands grabbing me holding me down, laughing in my face, as they carved into my skin. The pain...it hurt so much...I couldn't scream... the material from the gag dug into the sides of my mouth and I could only wait for it to be over... for the pain to stop... for it all to stop...

A hand clamped down on my arm and I screamed, jerking away from the touch.

Shhhh...it is all right. I will not hurt you.

My breaths came in heavy pants. I licked my lips and forced myself to take deep breaths. Ashamed of myself for having a panic attack at such an important moment, I closed my eyes and let myself bathe in the silence. The one thing that had come from losing my hearing was when it all became too much I could simply close my eyes and pretend like they were all gone. I was alone. There was no one there that could hurt me. Cal and Lu were far away. They couldn't get to me here.

To his credit, Ryu did not try to touch me again. In fact, he seemed to sit completely still until I calmed down. Then and only then did he shift on the bed, making it dip at my back. Opening my eyes, I twisted around in my seat trying, even though I knew I couldn't, to see him.

My hands searched the bed for a place to lie down. When my fingers brushed against something that was decidedly not the bed, I gasped. Smooth and somehow rough at the same time my hands traveled over the length of it until my fingers briefly brushed cloth and then that smoothness again.

I swallowed thickly.

I was touching the drake king.

I almost pulled my hands away. Then I cursed myself. Why was I so worried about touching the drake king, we'd just been more than intimate a few moments ago? In fact, remnants of it were still drying on my breast.

However, curiosity got the best of me and since Ryu was not stopping me, I continued my exploration. My fingers trailed along the ridges of his abdomen. The muscles there contracted under my touch and yet he did not pull away. Becoming more brave, I shifted so that I was fully kneeling beside him and pressed both my hands flat against the surface of his chest.

Ryu laid there and didn't move, allowing me to run my hands up and over his chest, where it moved up and down ever so slightly. I would never have known it had I not felt it beneath my hands. At least, he was alive. That didn't explain why he was letting me have my way with him.

His chest shook and I jerked my hands back. That was when I realized he was laughing at me.

What's so funny? I shoved the thought at him, trying not to think about the fact that I was indeed talking to someone in my head.

Two large hands covered my own. I tensed and waited. Only for Ryu to place them back onto his chest. *My apologies for laughing. Please proceed with having your way with me.*

I didn't know how but I knew he was smiling at me. And I found myself wishing I could see it. Shoving that thought aside, I moved my hands up his chest and over his broad shoulders before making my way back to his face. My fingertips slid over the line of his jaw and up to the pointed edge of his ears. I traced my fingers over the tip of them earning me a puff of air against my chest where I leaned over him. Curious at his reaction, I moved onto the rest of his face along the ridge of his nose and then the span of his eyes, along his eyebrows and then up to...his horns. My hands hesitated at the hardness protruding from the top of his head. What was it like to have horns? Did they hurt? Would he even feel it if I touched them?

I felt Ryu stiffen next to me as if waiting to see what I would do.

What the hell, I'd come this far might as well go all the way!

I found the base of the horns where the metal rings wrapped around them. Careful of the small spikes that decorated the rings, I moved over them and up the smooth length of them. They were different from the rest of him. Not as rough, more smooth to the touch and where I thought the tip would be sharp it didn't hurt when I slid my finger along the top of it. I moved my hand up and down them fascinated by the very existence of them until a hand caught both of mine in their grasp.

Frowning, I peered down at where I thought Ryu's face was.

I would not do that.

Staring at him for a moment, I tried to decipher what he meant. Then my eyes widened and I pulled my hands away from him, shoving them behind me. My earlier confidence had disappeared and I didn't think I could stomach anything remotely sexual in that moment.

Something slithered up along the top of my thighs and then pressed between them. Cold metal made me yelp and I jerked back. The thing pulled away at my reaction.

It took me a moment to realize it was the drake king's tail. When I did, my face heated for some unknown reason. Why had he touched me with it and why...why did I kind of like it?

Trying not to think too much about it, I laid on the bed and turned my back to Ryu. The room was chilly and I found myself shivering a few moments later. The bed shifted beside me and I tensed, expecting the drake king to go back on his word about bedding me, only to find a blanket being spread out over me.

Sighing, I snuggled into the warmth of it and closed my eyes. Soon, I was asleep and it was the soundest I had slept in months.

Chapter 6

Ryu

THE FEMALE HUMAN FELL ASLEEP faster than Ryu did and stayed that way long after he woke. Curled up against his side, the female had one leg thrown over his waist and her hands wrapped around his bicep. She sighed happily in her sleep, pressing her soft breasts against his arm, her leg shifting over his groin in her sleep. Against his will, Ryu's cock hardened and ached to sink into the softness beside him.

He remembered the feel of her lips wrapped around his cock not more than a few hours before. Ryu hadn't planned on letting the female anywhere near him until he figured out what exactly the human female wanted. To his surprise, Georgia seemed to have some kind of need to prove that she wasn't afraid of him. Though, once she had gotten started her stink of fear quickly morphed into the musky sweet scent of her arousal. It had only spurred him on more. Then there was the feel of her hot cavern around his length, the small sounds she made in the back of her throat while she gobbled him down. He'd never had such an enthusiastic partner who wasn't getting anything out of the exchange.

She shifted and sighed once more in her sleep. The woman must not hinder any ill will toward the drakes to be able to fall asleep in the enemy king's bed so easily, her previous action aside. Especially one as valuable as the Kinoko's princess.

Ryu stared down at the princess in the dark. His gaze slid over her prone form, from the long black braid that laid between them almost reaching down to her feet, to the bare shoulder that had escaped from her nightgown. His fingers itches to trace the exposed flesh. Ryu curled his fingers into a fist, gritting his teeth against the temptation.

Why had he let the female touch him like he had? The sexual act he understood. It was hard to think about saying no to a beautiful creature offering herself for his pleasure. But the touching afterward was an intimacy he never let anyone else have with him. If anyone else had touched him in that manner he would have burned them to a crisp. No one touched the king without his permission. Even those who sparred with him were afraid to touch him in the wrong manner less they felt his wrath. Female drakes, though they desired him, knew better than to try to come to him. He would let his brothers know if he wanted someone and they would bring them to his room much like they had brought the female.

Except she was so different from drake females or even the human females he'd met before. There was a strength in her that she tried to hide from him in their first meeting. He had known from the moment he had stepped into the gathering room who she was. Ryu had spies everywhere, even in the Kinoko's palace. Many of his enemies thought that because he was not human that his kind were beasts without thoughts and feelings. He had the wits enough to find out about the kingdom he dwelled in.

The moment he became king several decades ago, he had his informants provide him with images of all of the Kinoko's royals. However, he had not thought to have them updated or to find out any new information about the Kinoko's princess as of late. He didn't think it was important. They didn't bother him so he didn't bother them. It was the way they both liked it.

Ryu would be sure to remedy that soon. He had heard about the queen's death but it would have been nice to know that the Kinoko's princess had lost her hearing. It would have made their first encounter more pleasant. Now Ryu had to rethink the way he would approach this. He knew the princess wanted something from him. Ryu just needed to figure out what.

There was a kind of brokenness to her. A hesitancy that made herself conscious about her body. He'd seen it when she had tried to disrobe for him.

A sudden surge of rage poured into him and Ryu pulled back from the female. He had this sudden protectiveness in him for her that he had not felt for anyone other than his brothers. Even then he would rarely lift his claw to help. They would laugh at him for trying.

Scowling at the female, Ryu slipped out of the bed, making sure not to shake it and awaken the princess. He stepped back from the bed, his gaze lingering on her soft form for longer than he wanted to admit. His foot hit the armor he'd left on the floor the night before and a loud clang rang throughout the room.

Ryu froze.

Then he sagged as he remembered the princess couldn't hear him. With a slow release of breath, he bent down and picked up his armor, working on tying each piece into place while his eyes slid back to the princess of their own accord.

What kind of horrors had she gone through to offer herself to a creature she had just met? And one that had a bad reputation of their own? Did she think so little of herself that she didn't care who used her body? Or was there something else going on?

Either way, Ryu needed to speak to his brothers. He needed to get to the bottom of this before the princess woke and turned all their worlds upside down.

Once dressed, Ryu stalked toward the door. Pulling it open with one hand, Ryu glanced back over his shoulder at the princess once more who moaned and shifted in her sleep. His tail swung back and forth eager to curl back up into the bed with the soft body pressed against him. She was so much different than the drake women with their bodies as hard as their hearts.

Forcing his gaze from the princess, he practically threw himself out the door and into the hallway, closing the door firmly behind him. Two guards stood outside the door. He turned to them with a snarl. "No one goes in there. I want to know immediately when she awakens."

The guards jerked their heads in compliance, keeping their eyes on the wall beyond.

Without waiting for them to comply, Ryu turned on his heel and strode down the hallway, aiming for their private dining area. If his brothers were anywhere, it would be in there.

Before he reached the dining area Ryu could hear the rambunctious laughter of his brothers. Ryu pushed open the door to the dining area, the light of the torches filling the room with an orange glow. A fire crackled in the pit on the ground where his two brothers sat around on stone and wooden stools, the smoke wafting up into a hole in the ceiling.

"Ah, there he is!" Desmond lifted his mug in the air toward Ryu with a grin. "We were wondering when you would roll out of the sweet sweet embrace of the Kinoko princess. Come tell us, how was it? Does she taste as sweet as she looks?" He drank long from his mug before tossing it to the ground with a satisfied sigh.

Ira chuckled and sipped from his own mug, his one good eye rolling in his head. "You do not pay attention if you think that princess is anything but a vicious little beast. Come brother, show us your battle wounds. From the fiery look in her eyes I would say she's a biter." He flashed his fangs at Ryu, the suggestiveness written all over his face and words.

Ignoring both of their questions, Ryu walked over to the table set up against the stone wall and picked up a mug of his own, pouring the mead from the pitcher sitting next to it until the mug was filled to the brim. He drank deeply from the mug, draining it before slamming it down on the table.

"That bad huh?" Desmond chuckled.

Spinning around, Ryu threw the mug in his hand at his brother's head.

Desmond dodged it, his laughter growing. "Oh by the old ones, she has you all twisted up."

Ryu snarled, baring his fangs at his brother. "Shut up. No one has me twisted up. She is a means to an end, that is all.

Once we find out what she wants she will be useless to us and then we will get rid of her."

Ira continued to sip from his mug and arched the brow on his good eye. "So what does she want?"

"I have yet to find that out." Ryu picked up a plate and fiddled with a few items. Something prodded at his mind and he paused before randomly throwing them onto his plate and spinning around. "Stay out of my head or by the old ones I will show you why we are descendants of dragons."

"Now, now don't get in a tizzy. We just wanted to know how this simpering little princess somehow not only got your tail in a twist but somehow the great drake king couldn't even get the information he wanted out of her in one night?" Desmond grinned so hard Ryu hoped it cracked his jaw.

Grabbing his plate and mug, Ryu stomped over to the fire and plopped down on the nearest stool. "Georgia does not have my tail in a twist," Ryu snarled, ripping a chunk of meat off the bone on his plate and then gesturing at Desmond's tail. "You haven't stopped wagging your tail since you saw the females." Ryu couldn't say anything about his brother Ira's tail since it rarely moved in time with his emotions. The drake had more control over his tail than any drake Ryu had seen. Which made him a great interrogator and a pain in the ass to play against in knuckle bones.

"Oh, it's Georgia now?" Desmond chortled, reaching over to take a piece of meat from Ryu's plate. Ryu smacked his hand away with a low growl of warning.

"Where did you take the other female?" Ryu asked Desmond, trying to move the conversation away from his night with Georgia.

Desmond leaned back, propping himself up on his tail, his legs stretched out in front of him. "Aryn is the other female and she is quite chatty for someone who is supposedly afraid of us."

Ryu arched a brow, pausing his mug at his mouth. "She wasn't?" Curious. The handmaiden seemed far more likely to piss herself with fright than the princess. Perhaps talking was her fear response. "What did she say?" If he couldn't get anything out of the princess then maybe his brother had better luck.

"Unfortunately, nothing that will help us figure out why they were wandering around Grebe Forest. Though, she did happen to mention that the princess was engaged to the prince of Plumus. Who sounds like a real snart wattzle."

Jaw clenched tight, Ryu tried to keep his tail from showing the irritation that soared through him at the thought of the princess being engaged to any man. Then his mind connected what Desmond said to something he overheard in the princess's mind.

"What is the name of the prince there?" Ryu asked out loud, a sinking feeling beginning to develop in his stomach.

Unaware of Ryu's turmoil, Desmond snatched a piece of meat off Ryu's plate and shoved it into his mouth, saying through chews, "There's two of them, I believe." He sucked the juices off his fingers noisily.

"Which one is her betrothed?" Ryu gritted his teeth, two seconds away from smashing the plate over his brother's head.

Desmond cocked his head to the side and glanced off into the distance. "Uhhh...I think Luis or maybe it was Callahan." He shrugged as if it were nothing to worry about.

Luis and Callahan.

Lu and Cal.

The plate and mug cracked in his hands and crumbled to the ground. His brothers jerked back with astonishment. Ryu ignored them.

Those were the names Ryu had heard several times in Georgia's head. The thought of those two touching his princess...hold on...*his* princess...when did that happen? He's known this female for a total of one night and suddenly he was claiming her as his own? He had yet to even taste the sweet creaminess of her skin.

"By the old ones, Ryu, think a little louder." Ira winced, turning his head to the side.

Ryu dragged a hand between his horns. "Did the handmaiden — Aryn was it? — say anything of importance?"

Desmond stared at Ryu for a moment and Ryu didn't need to peek into his head to know what his brother was thinking about. He wouldn't linger on what he thought of the princess; it would only give his brothers more ammunition to use against him.

"Well?" Ryu prodded once more, getting impatient and wanting to check on the princess now that he knew more about her condition.

Desmond leaned his elbows onto his knees and turned his eyes to the fire. "There's not that much to tell. She might have talked a lot but not about anything important. The engagement was the only thing of interest and even that she seemed unhappy about."

"Why would they be unhappy about the engagement?" Ira interjected with a thoughtful frown. "I thought Plumus was a prosperous kingdom. I would imagine they would be happy to have an alliance with them with the state of the Kinoko's coffers."

Ryu hummed at the question. The state of the Kinoko's financials was something they discussed often. Worried that it would cause them to be taken over by another kingdom that was less than hospitable to the drakes. Not that the Kinokos were the most gracious rulers to them. They were a kingdom unto themselves inside of another ruler's lands. The fact that the Kinokos hadn't tried to run them out yet was all that kept them from being the same as all the other kingdoms. They were one attack away from being full blown enemies.

"Perhaps gold is not everything..." Ryu trailed off, staring down at the fire as if it had all the answers to his questions.

One of the guards came scurrying into the dining area. His hand gripped his staff tight enough that his red scales turned pink.

"What?" Ryu barked, turning from his brothers.

"Your majesty..." the guard glanced between the brothers before landing his gaze back on Ryu. His eyes locked with Ryu's and then dropped to his chest. "She's awake."

Chapter 7

BY THE GODS, WHY WAS my bed so comfortable today? I didn't remember it being this nice when I went to bed last night. Hmmm...it's still dark out, just five more minutes. Aryn will come get me if I sleep too long. I sighed and snuggled further into the blankets, the scent of burning wood and rain filling my nostrils.

My eyes flew open.

Everything came back to me.

This wasn't my bed.

Sitting up straight in the bed, I tried to no avail to see in the darkness of the bedroom. I was in the drake king's bed.

And I had touched the drake king all over last night.

My hands came to my cheeks as they heated in memory. Then my fingers lowered to my lips, the taste of him still lingering there. I can't believe I did that. Why hadn't I taken the out Ryu had offered? I could have done this another way. He seemed like an understanding king, I was sure that was some way we could come to a mutual understanding that would allow me to get what I wanted without getting further into an entanglement with the drake king.

While it hadn't been an unpleasant experience, my thighs pressed together in remembrance of the encounter, and the drake king was nothing like I expected him to be. I thought he would be more along the lines of Cal and Lu, taking what he wanted, the consequences be damned. But Ryu...

Fuck...Ryu...he'd been gruff of course but understanding. He hadn't made me feel ashamed of my scars. He didn't even mention them. However, I could do without the extra coddling because of my disability. I might be unable to hear but I wasn't an invalid. He'd figure that out soon enough, I'd make sure of it.

Thinking of the drake king again caused me to freeze in place.

I glanced over toward his side of the bed where in the darkness I assumed he still slept. The bed didn't shift with him and I couldn't feel any body heat coming off of him. Did drake's have body heat or were they more like lizards? I tried to remember last night what he felt like...and that led to me feeling all sorts of strange feelings that had my core ache with need.

No. He'd been...hot. As if there were some kind of fiery core in his center. It must be nice not having to worry about getting cold. I shivered in place, wrapping the blanket tighter against me. I would freeze down here in the mountains if I had to live here all the time.

At the curious stillness from Ryu's side of the bed, I mustered up the courage to slide my foot over to his side. My foot searched out the drake king's leg only to find a cool spot in his absence.

Frowning, I reached out and patted the place next to me on the bed. Empty. Where had he gone? Why did I care? The bed was cool enough that the drake king couldn't have just left. He'd been gone for a little while.

Which was just... great. He left me here all alone in the dark. How the hell was I supposed to get out of this room let alone the bed by myself?

Scowling, I threw the blanket off of me and immediately regretted it. Tossing my legs over the side of the bed, I grabbed the blanket and wrapped it around myself before standing. Which direction was the door? If the bed was here and then the end of it was there...then that meant the door must be that way.

Slowly, I made my way across the dark room making sure to lift the blanket so I didn't trip over it. Unfortunately, I was so focused on not tripping on the blanket that I didn't feel the side table until my hip smacked into it.

I yelped and grabbed the offending piece of furniture before rubbing the sore spot on my hip. That was sure to leave a bruise. Well, what was one more? Couldn't make my body any worse.

Groaning, I inched my way forward more carefully now, one hand out in front of me to feel for any obstructions in my way. Time seems to go on forever when you are walking in the dark. I almost thought I had gotten turned around by the time my hand found the door. My hand trailed over the wood until it found the handle. Jerking it open, I found myself facing two drakes each with a look of concern on their faces.

"Are you all right?" the first one asked, his lips moving slowly and precisely. His scales were a silvery hue that almost shone like a rainbow in the torch light. It was actually kind of pretty though it did clash a bit with the yellowness of his eyes.

Holding the blanket tighter to me, I pointed back into the room. "Can I get some light in here? I can't see a damn thing."

The silver scaled drake glanced at the other one, a dark red scaled drake. The red drake shook his head. "We are not allowed to enter the room."

I gaped at him. "Not even to light the torches?"

The red drake frowned at me. "We do not disobey his majesty's orders. No one is allowed to enter the room."

I shot a look at the silver one who inclined his head in agreement. "Well then where is His Majesty?"

The two guards exchanged looks and I wanted to smack them both over the head.

"We can't tell you that," guard one said with a stiff upper lip.

Tightening the blanket around me, I stepped out of the bedroom, only to be stopped by both guards. "What? I can't leave?"

The guards exchanged a look again, this time the red one answered, "Well, he did not say you couldn't...only that no one could enter and for us to let him know when you were awake."

I had a hard time following what he said and ended up squinting at him by the end of it. Hopefully I got the gist which gave me enough leeway to do what I wanted.

"Then that means you can't stop me from leaving." I shoved past both of them, the two guards standing dumbfounded while I stalked down the hallway. I had no idea where I was going but I wasn't going to stand in that bedroom for a moment longer in the dark. If they couldn't come in and light the torches then I would just go out.

The red guard hustled the opposite way, not stopping me from leaving but the silver one came up to my side and kept pace with my movements. I glared up at him. "I don't need a babysitter."

The drake shrugged. "I don't want to lose my head for letting you wander around alone."

I bobbed my head and turned my gaze forward though I had no idea where I was going. At that thought, I stopped in place and turned to the silver drake. "What's your name?"

The drake glanced over my head and then down at me. I stared hard at his lips. Yet I could not figure out what he was saying. Tawin? Tatoon? I shook my head and sighed. This was going to be harder than I thought to hide my disability.

Fuck it.

I gestured with my hands while saying aloud. "Can you spell that?"

The drake looked down at my hands and cocked his head to the side for a moment, then his eyes widened. He touched his free hand to his ear and then pointed at me, his mouth moving slowly, "You can't hear?"

I flushed and wrapped the blanket tighter around me, my eyes going to the ground. Then I scowled cursing at myself for allowing some guard to make me feel bad about myself. I lifted my eyes and stared the drake down. "No, I can't. So what?"

Pursing his lips, the drake pulled at the white braid going down his back. "This makes things difficult."

I shoved at his chest. "No, it doesn't. Just read my mind."

Eyes wide, the drake shook his head. "No, no. I cannot do that. Only the drake king and his brothers have that ability."

I blew out a breath through my lips. "Fine. Just talk slowly and where I can see your mouth."

Jerking his head up and down once, the drake paused for a moment and stared up at the ceiling before turning his gaze back to me. "You can call me..." he paused thinking for a moment before saying where I could see his mouth clearly, "Tat."

"Tat?" I frowned at the drake, saying the word over in my mouth several times before grinning. "Alright, Tat it is."

"Where are you going?" Tat asked, taking careful measures to speak slowly for me to read his lips. "It is not safe for you to wander around alone."

I grinned at the drake, holding the blanket tight around me. "Well, I have you so I'll be safe enough." I paused and glanced back down the corridor. "And I'm looking for my handmaiden, Aryn? Do you know where they took her?"

Tat bobbed his head. "I can take you to her."

"You can?" I grinned broadly and looped my arm through the drake's. "Then by all means lead the way."

Still a bit cautious of me, Tat led me down the hallway and toward a different part of the mountain than from last night. I wondered where they were keeping Aryn. I hoped they were treating her right. If they weren't there was going to be hell to pay. I tightened my hand on the drake's arm and clung tighter to him. If it bothered him, he didn't say so.

There were several drakes coming and going as we walked past yet still no females. Figuring that I could ask Tat about it once we found Aryn, I kept my questions and assumptions to myself. Patience was something I was proficient at after all. Everything usually reveals itself on their own whether they want to or not.

We walked for several more minutes before we stopped outside a set of double doors. The first curiosity was the two guards standing on either side of the doors. I understood guarding Aryn but these two didn't seem the type to guard a single little human woman. They were humongous. Larger than any of the drakes I'd seen so far and that included the drake king.

Both of them were dark scaled, one more of onyx color while the other a deep blue. They were bald and their horns were so long that they curved over the back of their heads. Their heads turned in one at our approach. The eyes that stared us down were almost as dark as their skin, completely different from any of the drakes I'd seen so far. The firmness of their expressions made my footsteps falter. Tat had to tug on my arm slightly to get me to keep moving forward.

I swallowed and blinked at the two of them, trying to not focus on the sharp spikes pointing out of each piece of their armors. Their swords at their sides and backs were so malicious looking that I suddenly wished that Ryu was there.

Tat patted my hand and glanced down at me with a reassuring look. I gave him a weak smile in return as we stopped before the two guards. They didn't immediately move out of the way for us to pass them, instead each of them looked me over with slow consideration. They seemed to take no notice of Tat who was far more intimidating and dangerous than me.

The blueish one's lips moved addressing Tat but his eyes on me. "What is it doing here?"

Tat stiffened.

I forced my gaze away from the drake to Tat whose mouth moved slowly. "She wishes to see her friend."

"Does it have permission?" The drake narrowed his eyes on me, his mouth pressed into a thin line.

I was starting to not like this drake. Not waiting for Tat to answer for me, I stepped forward and shoved my finger at the drake's chest. "It has a name. And I want to see my friend. So move!"

The drake bared his teeth at me, his fangs glinting maliciously. I scowled back at him. He was just trying to scare me and I wouldn't be scared away. I wanted to see

Aryn. I had to make sure she was alright. I would not let this big drake deter me.

"Let me pass now."

The darker of the two drakes stepped closer to me and I held my ground. "We are not allowed to let anyone in without the king's permission. It is not anything against you, it is just the rules."

I stared at the drake's mouth and frowned. No one? No one could go in without the drake king's permission? What the hell was in there? On the other hand, at least this drake seemed to be the more reasonable of the two. The first one was being considerably uncouth. I couldn't stand bullies. I had enough of them with Cal and Lu. I would not abide by anyone not letting me do what I wanted to do just because they said so.

"Then how do I get the king's permission?" I gripped the blanket closer to me and took a step back, giving us all a bit of breathing room. The two drakes exchanged a look with each other before peering back down at me.

"You must petition the king for permission and then wait the appropriate amount of time to be able to enter," the darker of the two drake's explained.

I gaped at them. "Appropriate amount of waiting time? How long is that?"

They shrugged.

Tat answered, turning slightly so that I could read his lips. "Depends on the king's mood. Sometimes it is a few days, sometimes weeks."

I frowned and stared at the door perplexed. "What exactly is in there?"

"The female quarters," the blueish one stated bluntly. "You would be in there as well if the king had not claimed you as his."

I bristled at that. Claimed me as his indeed. I was no one's property.

"Well, I am a guest here. And my friend is in there." I pointed with one finger, holding the blanket tight with the other. "I demand to see my friend right now."

"That's not going to happen." The dark one gripped his staff tightly, his face unyielding.

It seemed as if I was not going to win this one. I couldn't back down though. I had to make sure that Aryn was alright. I'd dragged her into this after all. If something happened to her...

The air in the corridor tingled and the ground slightly vibrated. The guards in front of me fell to one knee, their heads lowered. Even Tat went down to the ground. Peering curiously down at them, I wondered what was going on. I didn't have to wonder for long. A moment later, the drake king walked around the corner.

Chapter 8

Ryu

STANDING BEFORE THE DOORS TO the female's quarters was the Kinokos princess. Barely concealed in the blanket she had no doubt pulled from his bed, Ryu's nostrils flared at the sign of the drakes around her. The contempt the drakes had for the female human before them was easily deciphered without having to delve into their heads. Tatoween, one of the guards Ryu had left to watch over the sleeping princess was the only one not thinking about the annoying disturbance the female was creating.

The princess herself stared down at the guards in wary confusion before those chestnut colored eyes flicked up and locked with Ryu's. Her small hand tightened on the blanket around her slim shoulders, her large breasts barely contained within their confines even with the thin fabric of her night gown beneath. Ryu shoved the thought back. This was no time to be focusing on the strange attraction he had to the princess. Not when he had yet to get to the bottom of why she and her ladies maid had been in his forest.

"What's going on here?" Ryu commanded, stopping before the lot of them. The guard who had informed him of the princess's waking scurried up behind him but wisely kept silent.

None of the guards answered at first, then Tatoween slowly lifted his head. Hesitantly he slid his gaze up to Ryu's before dipping it back down to Ryu's chin. "Your majesty, our guest wishes to see her friend and insists she could not wait until your return. I brought her here as she requested. However..." his eyes flicked over at the two guards who stayed knelt on the ground.

The bluish one, Cadben, head jerked up at Tatoween's words, his eyes narrowed at the other drake. Jaw clenched, Cadben growled out, "It is against the law to allow anyone...regardless of who they are...into the female's quarters without the king's permission."

"As you are correct," Ryu shifted his attention from the drake's to the increasingly peeved princess. "I do believe we can make an exception for this instance." Making a decision, Ryu bobbed his head in Georgia's direction. "Yes, I hereby declare that Georgia, the princess of Kinoko, may enter the females' quarters whenever she likes without asking for permission."

Cadben's mouth gaped and his thoughts gave away his need to protest. Ryu let out a warning growl at the drake, prompting him to immediately drop his head back down in prostration.

Crossing his arms with self-satisfaction, Ryu waited for the princess to cry out her happiness and praise him with adoration for helping her without asking for anything in return. That wasn't the case.

Georgia's eyes narrowed into slits, her lips twisted to one side, and her fingers tightened so tightly that Ryu could see her little hands shaking with what he had hoped would be unadulterated happiness...wishful thinking on his part.

Slipping into her mind was easier than anyone else's.

What in the ever loving goddesses do you think you are doing?

Ryu cocked his head to the side, his lips pursed tightly so his fang pinched into his flesh. Seeing that this was going to turn into a fight, Ryu glanced pointedly at the drakes and let out a low rumbling growl. The drakes stiffened. When they didn't move Ryu drew heat into his throat, steam coming out of his nostrils and slipping out between his clenched teeth. The sight of the trickling smoke was enough of a warning for the three drakes to draw up to their feet and stalk out of the corridor as quickly as they could.

Tatoween glanced back at the princess briefly. But one snuff of a growl from Ryu and he scurried away, leaving Ryu alone with the glowering princess.

How can you possibly be angry with me now? Ryu closed the distance between the two of them until he towered over the Kinoko princess. *You wished to see your friend. I have granted you the ability to do so.*

Oh thank you, most gracious king. Georgia mockingly bowed at the waist, one hand holding the blanket while the other flounced out to the side with a flick of her fingers. *For allowing me to see the person I came here with. For not keeping me in the same room as you keep all your other whores.*

Anger swept through Ryu. He stepped closer to Georgia causing her to jerk back from him with wide startled eyes. He kept stalking her until her back hit the dirt wall of the corridor and his breath hit the top of her head, blowing her dark hair around her face. *We are not human. We do not abide by your rules. If you wish to keep your life, you will show respect to the females of this kingdom. Or you will not live to see your friend again.*

Georgia blinked up at Ryu. The rapid beat of her pulse fluttered in Ryu's ears. She licked her lips, her head bouncing off the wall as she tried to look up at him. Her chest heaved, her breasts straining against the material of the nightgown, the blanket having fallen to the ground between their feet. The rage pouring through his veins slowed and was quickly replaced with another feeling all together.

Ryu reached a hand out and cupped the side of her face, his clawed finger tracing along her jawline and then the line of her lips. Georgia's mouth dropped open, her breath tickling his finger tips. Staring down into her eyes, Ryu leaned forward the overwhelming urge to taste the fire in the words the little princess kept shouting into his head leading his actions. A flicker of fear touched his head. Ryu lowered his hand, releasing a long breath.

Taking a step back from the princess, Ryu gestured to the side. After you, princess.

Georgia stared at him a moment then she blinked her eyes rapidly, her mouth clipping shut into a grim line. Without a parting thought, she reached down and grabbed the blanket off the ground, gripping it to her chest as she stalked toward the double doors. She didn't wait for Ryu as she shoved the doors open with one hand, both of them slamming against the walls of the interior room, not that she noticed.

The female drakes shot to their feet, their weapons drawn. In the midst of them stood the small older human female. Paying no mind to the armed drakes, Georgia rushed toward her lady's maid. The female drakes started in a combination of surprise and confusion as the little woman rushed toward them before they registered Ryu's presence.

"Your highness," the female cried out, grabbing for the princess and pulling her into a tight embrace.

A tail brushed against Ryu's leg, sliding up the length of his calf. Ryu's eyes skittered over to the female drake who knelt near his feet. The deepish purple of her scales flickered in the light of the flame torches. The female had clearly bathed recently, and the hint of rosemary wafting into his nostrils told him she was waiting for his arrival.

"Daylea," Ryu greeted.

Having been acknowledged, the female drake slid to her knees and caressed her claws along Ryu's calf and up the side of his thigh. "I was wondering when you might come by to see me."

"Not now," he grunted in response, shaking the female's hands from his leg and refocusing on the two humans.

Withdrawing from the princess, the human female held Georgia out from herself to look over the princess, spinning her around in place as if she were not insulting Ryu with her actions. "Are you alright?"

Georgia peered over her shoulder at Ryu, her lashes fluttering against her cheeks and a pink tint lighting her skin. Instead of answering with the voice Ryu knew she had, Georgia made several quick gestures with her hands, moving over her face and then body.

Brows furrowed, Ryu stepped further into the room. The drake females lowered their weapons, each of them falling to one knee as he passed. Ryu ignored them, watching the two humans exchange a series of hand movements in rapid succession. A few female drakes chanced a look at the two humans with curious eyes before dropping their gazes back to the ground.

He knew they were talking about him. Yet the princess was gesturing too fast for him to read her mind and figure out what she was saying.

Ryu huffed and stroked a hand over his jaw. This wouldn't do. Not at all.

"What are you saying?" Ryu commanded, stopping before the two small humans.

Georgia slowly turned to him, raising a brow as she crossed her arms under her breasts, her lips ticking up on one side. *Not much fun not knowing what someone is saying, is it?*

Ryu opened his mouth to retort and then clipped it shut. He couldn't argue with that. Ryu felt the eyes of the drake females settle on him with wary interest.

"Your majesty," the human female stepped forward, shooting a warning look at the princess. "I apologize for leaving you out of the conversation. I'm sure you can understand that because of my charge's condition that it is easy for her to fall back into what is most comfortable for her. We meant no disrespect to you or the other drakes." She swept an arm around the room, getting a round of appreciative looks from the female drakes.

Ryu pinged his eyes from the smaller woman before him and then to the princess and back, arching a brow at the princess in turn. He could see that the handmaiden was used to speaking for her charge and Georgia was more than happy to let her take the lead. However, the way that Ryu responded to the woman after she had clearly won over the female drakes would say much about him.

The human princess had thought on more than one occasion that he was barbaric in keeping the women all together and away from the men. What the fiery little princess didn't know was that if he didn't keep the females away from the males, he wouldn't have any males left alive.

Not that the males fought over the females. No, no. No drake female would allow a male to fight over her. There were far more males than females in their kingdom and all a female had to do was crook her tail and the males would come running, ready to do her bidding.

It was far more for everyone's safety than just to keep the females in their place.

Blowing out the hot steam that billowed in his throat, Ryu let out the need to reprimand the female. "I do not believe we have been properly introduced. I am Ryu, king of the drakes, and you are?"

Georgia snorted.

The female grabbed Georgia's arm in a tight grip, making the princess wince. "My name is Aryn. And you have made my charge's acquaintance, Georgia. We thank you for your hospitality." Georgia made another distinctive sound of disbelief. "And we wish nothing more than to be out of your hair and get back to our kingdom so that you and yours can go back to your business." She smiled tightly at the female drakes around them.

Georgia grabbed Aryn by the arm and scowled at her, gesturing quickly at her handmaiden.

Unsure what they were discussing so rapidly, Ryu interrupted with a wave of his hand. "I cannot let you leave. You have been to our home and we cannot risk having others find it."

Georgia looked pointedly at Aryn and jerked a hand in his direction as if to say see.

Aryn scowled before turning her gaze to Ryu. "So we are to be your prisoners forever? Just because we wandered into the wrong part of the forest?" She crossed her arms over her chest and frowned. "If you treated every trespasser that way there would be quite a lot more humans wandering around." She made a show of skimming her eyes around the room. "And as I can see we are very much lacking any familial resemblance here, do you?"

Ryu stepped up to her with a vicious smile. "Trespassers are usually killed. Would you prefer that? Because it could be arranged."

To his pleasure, the handmaiden paled and visibly swallowed.

Georgia squeezed her hand and then turned her gaze to Ryu. "We'll stay." Picking at her gown, she grimaced. "Clothes?"

One glance down at her nightgown and last night shoved itself back into his mind. The image of her kneeling before him her gown crumpled up on the floor between them as she swallowed down his cock.

Ryu jerked his head toward Beautine. "Take care of it." Then without another word, he spun on his heels and stalked out of the room.

He had to get out of there before he threw the little princess down in the middle of the female quarters and took her the way the dragons did of old.

Chapter 9

I WATCHED THE DRAKE KING stalk out of the room as if the underworld itself was nipping on his heels.

It took a moment for the female drakes to relax enough to come back to their feet. When they did they all turned toward Aryn and me. My body froze, the full attention of the room on myself not making it easy to celebrate my accomplishment. Somehow the female drakes were more menacing than the males had been. Their eyes glinted with a mysterious glow. I couldn't tell if they were thinking about how they could help me or what I tasted like. In my wariness, I inched closer to Aryn.

Aryn smiled at me and patted me on the shoulder before saying to the room while she signed to me. "You can rest easy here, princess. These drakes will not harm you."

As if to prove her point, a pale female drake, her scales and skin the color of honey dew, stepped toward us.

The female drakes had the same features as the males if only softer in some way. Their hair they kept in all fashions, some short, others so long that they had to braid it to keep it from touching the floor like the female coming toward us. However, unlike the males, the women wore more clothing but not by a lot. This female's chest was covered with the same type of cloth that the males used for their lower half. Many of them wore the same kind of fashioned top half with the straps going over each shoulder and connecting at the back of the neck. The most curious part about their clothing wasn't the exposed skin but the armor they wore. Did the females fight alongside the males? Or was the armor for show?

The female drake held a clawed hand out to me and offered me a welcoming smile. "I am Beautine." I read from her lips. "Welcome. We are pleased to meet a friend of Aryn's."

Curious how my lady's maid had gained the trust of the female drakes so quickly, I warily laid my much smaller hand in that of the drake's. "Georgia," I said out loud. My eyes slid over to Aryn, wondering what exactly I was supposed to do now.

I would like to find something else to wear. The nightgown I was wearing wasn't exactly meant for such activities. As it were it would have to be thrown away. There was no way it was salvageable with all the rips and dirt and goddess knows what else from rolling around in the stables before.

"Go," Aryn gestured to Beautine and signed to me, "go with her and she will find you something else to wear." She swept a hand over her own clothing which had been replaced with a similar style to that of Beautine in a dark blue. Aryn's top covered just above her belly button. However, the drakes did not seem to be quite as self-conscious about their exposed skin as Aryn did who kept trying to hide the visible slice of flesh with her hands and arms.

Reluctantly, I followed Beautine to the back part of the room where there were several other openings. The one that

Beautine led me through ended up being a bathroom of sorts. The sight of a bathtub almost made me cry out in relief. I wanted nothing more than to strip out of these clothes and wash the night off of me and the lingering scent of the drake king that clung to my skin and continued to assault my nose.

Though excited to bathe, I made myself calm down. With the way the drakes' lived I couldn't hope for anything more than clean water. I'd be lucky if the water wasn't freezing.

Beautine had one hand on my lower back, ushering me toward the tub. I hesitated at the side of the tub, watching as the drake flipped a knob that two seconds later caused water to come pouring out of a metal tube and into the tub. I leaned closer to the tub, curious about the manner in which they were filling their bathtub. Cautiously, I dipped my fingers into the water expecting it to be cold and found it pleasantly warm.

I spun around and grinned a genuine smile at Beautine, who smiled in return. It took me back the fanged grin but I told myself that it wasn't a threatening smile. They couldn't help the fangs in their mouth looked so menacing. Beautine gestured toward the tub with an eager claw and said, "Go ahead."

Still I hesitated.

Stripping bare for the drake king had been one thing. I'd been pissed off and wanted to prove a point. Even if I hadn't had to go through with it.

However, now with the female drake watching me, shame and uncertainty clouded my mind. I clung to the nightgown around me and pondered how to ask for some privacy without sounding rude.

Beautine stepped toward me and reached out. I flinched back from her touch and shook my head, holding my night gown to myself. Beautine stopped and dropped her hand, her brows furrowing together. Then some light came on in her eyes. She stepped around me and grabbed a wooden box with several glass bottles inside of it. Holding them out to me, she pushed them into my hands and then turned on her heel and left.

Looking down at the box in my hands, I turned it this way and that, watching the liquids inside move. Leaning forward, I sniffed the bottles. Finding them pleasantly full of floral scents, I shifted around to the bathtub. I found a small ledge near the tub's lip to sit the box and stripped the filthy nightgown off. I balled it up and tossed it to the side.I never wanted to touch that thing again.

I sank into the tub with a long sigh. Rubbing my hands over my skin, I splashed some water in my face and over my hair. My fingers caught on the tangles in my hair and I winced. I slowly extracted my fingers, and reached for the box of cleaning products. I found one that smelled like lilacs and poured it into my hair. Scrubbing the liquid through my hair, I tried to focus on getting clean and what was going to happen next.

What was going to happen next?

I needed the drake king to agree to help me. The only thing was, how exactly would Ryu help and what would he want in return? My body remembered how it felt to be pressed up against the big hot body of the drake king and I would be lying if I didn't say a part of me wanted him to demand me follow through with my previous offer.

What in the world was wrong with me? I scrubbed myself with the scented oil until my skin turned red and stung. Scowling at how worked up I was letting myself get over a beast of a male, I dunked my whole body under the water, letting the water encase my thoughts and worries.

I stayed under the water waiting for that telltale sign of my breath running out when a vibration shot through the water.

My eyes flipped open. A watery figure stood over the tub. I gasped, taking in a lung full of water and jerked up. Coughing, I gripped the sides of the tub and blinked at the concerned face of Beautine.

Beautine patted me on the back, helping me get the water out of my lungs. I waved her off and stood from the tub. I realized my mistake the second Beautine took a step back from me.

Holding a towel in one hand, her eyes unabashedly moved over my body. Her eyes found the most recent of Cal's collection of atrocities against my flesh and narrowed. Beautine's mouth opened and then after a second thought, closed and shook her head. She gestured for me to come forward, the towel open for me to step into.

Curious by her lack of speech, I let her wrap the towel around me and then stepped away from her and said with my hands as well as my voice, "You do not need to be silent. I can read your lips if you speak in my eyesight."

Beautine's brows rose, a strange sight on a drake face. "I did not want to cause you undue confusion."

I grinned and chuckled. "I thank you for that but it is unnecessary. I have learned to survive."

The female drake inclined her head. "As have we all." Turning from me, she picked up the crimson bundle of clothing she must have brought in with her. "Here. For you."

I grasped the bundle in my hands. "Thank you."

Jerking her head once in reply, Beautine left without another word.

Curious to see what Beautine had given me, I unfolded the crimson fabric, the material shifting in my hand as if it were made of water. There were two pieces. One part was a long skirt that went well past my feet —drakes were generally a lot taller than humans — I ended up having to roll it at the top to keep myself from tripping on it. The top part had far less material to go with it than the bottom. When I slipped it over my head, I found my breasts were barely contained by material making the top part of my outfit a bit more obscene than I was used to.

With no further choice in the matter, I found the shoes I had come in and slipped them on. They didn't match the outfit but they also wouldn't be seen beneath the long skirt. Not that I thought the drakes cared about my style choices. I was simply ecstatic to be out of my dirty nightgown.

It wasn't Beautine who came for me but Aryn.

Happy for the chance to speak to my friend alone, I gestured with my hands rapidly. "Are you okay?"

Aryn pursed her lips. "I said I was. The drake females are not the brutes, the males are. They have been more than courteous."

"Not all of the males are brutes." I signed in return. "A guard who helped me find you was more than friendly. Though, I cannot say the same for their king."

Lifting her hands to reply, Aryn paused and then dropped them with a heave of her shoulders. Taking me by the shoulders, Aryn drew me into a tight embrace. Confused by the sudden hug, I wrapped my arms around her back, holding her to me until she released me a moment later.

"I wish I could have protected you from all this." Aryn said with her mouth and her hands, her eyes tearing at the edges. "You should never have had to suffer the way you have. What would your mother say?"

With a grim smile, I swiped her tears with my thumbs. "She would say that our people come first and our suffering second. I can only do what I think is right and hope for the best."

Aryn scowled. "We will do more than hope. How do you plan to get the drake king's help?"

I pursed my lips and then signed reluctantly. "I do not know how to bring it up to him but I do know that I need to gather their trust first before asking for anything."

"It's not as if you can seduce him into helping you," Aryn gestured with a smirk.

I paused for a moment and then remembered the taste of the drake king in my mouth the way his grip tightened in my hair as I swallowed him down. Maybe I could seduce them into helping me.

"Georgia," Aryn signed and said aloud, her hands grabbing my arms. "What are you thinking, child?"

"I think just that—"

"You think what?" Aryn asked before I turned away from her.

I had to make the drake king want me, to crave me more than life itself so that my request will not be such a large one. He will want to help me because he can't live without me. I will make sure of it.

Beautine appeared in the room once more, stopping me in my tracks. "The king has requested your presence. Both of you."

Chapter 10

Cal

MONTHS AND YEARS OF PLANNING. Of gathering their forces, making friends with the Kinokos so they would trust them. Just so that they could get to the point of offering their hand to the princess.

For what? Cal thought as he sat at the table in his bedroom, drinking deeply from his glass. The amber liquid burned his throat as it went down. Nothing. Absolutely nothing.

What a waste.

The woman in his lap tried to gain his attention, wiggling over his cock like the whore she was. Cal wasn't in the mood. His thoughts were firmly on the princess that had slipped through his fingers.

Cal thought the princess was going to be easy. Especially when he had heard about the princess's misfortune. The sickness had spread through Plumus as well but it had not affected them so much as the Kinokos. Their queen's death was a fortunate event for the Kinokos. It made the Kinoko king weak and easy to manipulate into becoming allies with them.

Before then the Kinoko king had been hesitant, seeing the Plumus as too aggressive, too brutal in their doings. Now, though, with his queen gone and his daughter broken, the Kinoko's king had no choice but to take the first offer of alliance he could get. Even more so now that the kingdom was growing poorer by the minute.

Plumus would save them from being invaded by another kingdom. There were already stirrings to the west. Biding their time before they took the chance to take over the Kinokos. The only thing keeping them from attacking right now was the threat of the drake who lived in the wilds of the Kinoko's land.

The fucking drakes. The scourge of the land. Those half breed monstrosities should have been wiped out long ago. It would be the first of Cal's duties once he took over this penniless kingdom. Dragons. Magic. Nonsense. All of those were a waste of space. Resources that could be better used elsewhere. He would not make the same mistake the Kinoko's king has made. He would not be lenient or passive in his rule.

Except all his plans meant absolutely nothing now that the princess was missing. How that even happened was beyond him. Didn't they have guards? Measures set in place so that the princess was kept under lock and key? Who just let the heir to the throne do as they pleased?

A burning rage filled Cal at how the little princess had escaped right under his fucking nose.

"That bitch doesn't know who she's dealing with," Cal slammed his glass down on the table in his bedroom, scowling at the wall before him. The woman in his lap eeped and shifted in his lap to get off. Cal tightened his grip on her waist and glowered. The woman instantly stopped moving.

His brother, Luis, rotated his own glass between his hands, leaning over in his chair hands and head lowered. "We do not even know if the princess is responsible for her disappearance. For all we know she could have been kidnapped."

Cal snorted. "With her handmaiden and their horses? Doubtful." Cal shoved the woman off his lap, tired of her constant weeping and turned to his brother. "No, that little bitch knew exactly what she was doing. She's making a fool of us and I won't abide by it."

Luis straightened and sat his glass on the table. "Perhaps we played with her too much too soon. We should have shown more restraint. Waited until after the wedding."

Rolling his eyes, Cal downed the last of the liquid in his glass before answering, "How was I to know that she'd choose herself over her kingdom. Everything pointed to her being an easy target and it's not like you were telling me to stop." He smirked at his brother, remembering the lovely color of red that spilled from the princess's flesh as they carved her up. "You enjoyed every bit of it as much as I did."

"Still," Luis placed his glass on the table and picked up the decanter, filling the glass back up. "In light of the new situation, we must try to refrain from causing any more stirring. The king is already too suspicious as it is."

Cal arched a brow at his brother. "And what is it you are suggesting?"

Luis's lips curled up into a vicious smile. "That you play the part of the distraught betrothed and gather your soldiers."

Frowning at his brother's suggestion, Cal crossed one leg over the other and twisted the glass in his hand. "You want me to start a war to find her? Who would I even be fighting against?"

Shrugging, a sly glint shone in Luis's eyes. "Whoever you want. Either way it gives us an excuse to bring our men into the Kinokos kingdom without causing further suspicion, putting us one step closer to taking this land for ourselves."

Cal hummed and tapped his fingers on the table with his free hand. "That is a good point. However...that still doesn't solve the problem of where the princess is right now."

"Oh, I wouldn't worry too much about that. If she has indeed run away, I have no doubt that she will make herself known eventually. A woman like that will not let her kingdom suffer for her actions for long. Not without a plan."

"And what plan is that?"

Luis tipped his glass to his lips, taking a sip of his drink before smacking and licking his lips. "Only time will tell, my brother. However, I think we can handle one little broken princess, don't you?"

Cal leaned back in his chair and stroked his chin, his fingers curling into his mustache, pulling the hairs until the pain became apparent. "Hmmm, that remains to be seen. I do not think we should be so quick to underestimate our little princess. She has far more bite than we thought and we do not want those teeth to find their way firmly in our asses."

Chapter 11

TAT WAS THERE AT THE entrance to the females' quarters to lead us to where the drake king had disappeared to. He kept his gaze forward and his mouth closed. Quite different from the drake I had spoken to just moments before. Someone must have been reprimanded for his loose lips.

"Where are we going?" I asked, speaking with my hands as well as my mouth.

Tat shot me a sideways look and began speaking, then stopped and turned to me pausing us in the corridor and started again, "The king has requested your presence in the dining area. I am to take you to him and his brothers." Then he turned and started walking again without waiting for my reply.

Irritated by the lack of emotion that came from the explanation, I followed after Tat while shooting a scowl at Aryn. This couldn't be good. I thought I had started to make a friend here but it seems I have been thwarted.

Aryn gripped my hand and squeezed meaningfully. I squeezed back and gave what I thought was a hopeful smile.

This was my idea after all. I didn't want her to think I was backing down now. This had to work or we would be doomed.

We passed the drake king's bedroom on the way to the dining area and I had the sudden urge to duck inside and hide. I shoved that urge down and lifted my chin. I'd face the drake king with my head held high. I had to gain their trust and to do that I had to spend more time with them. I couldn't very well seduce him if I wasn't near enough to fuck.

The dining area was not much more than a hole in the wall. Dirt floor, a table to the left filled with plates of food — my stomach rumbled in response — and a small fire in the middle of the floor where several stone seats were placed around it. On three of those seats sat the two drakes who had come in before the drake king the night before, each of them glancing in my direction with a mixture of curiosity and wariness. On the last seat sat Ryu, looking every bit as intimidating as he had a few moments ago.

Neither Ryu or the brothers stood at my entrance, either because they didn't find my presence important or it wasn't a custom of the drakes. Either way it made me feel tiny and insignificant. Throwing my shoulders back, I shoved that feeling away. I needed to exude confidence to get what I wanted. If I wilted then who knew what they would do to me.

Ryu's head lifted from the mug in his hand. I felt his eyes roam over my body, taking in every inch of the figure the crimson cloth showed off. The only reaction Ryu had was a slight flaring of his nostrils. His brothers were not so unresponsive in their assessment of me. They openly leered and licked their lips, their fangs peeking out with the action.

Tat stopped a few feet away from them, I shifted my position until I was able to see the drake guard's mouth as he spoke. "Your majesty, the prisoners."

I shot Tat a sharp look before turning that look onto the drake king. "Are we prisoners now?"

Ryu rose from his seat and approached. "You have not proven otherwise that we can trust you to be anything else."

My lips ticked up at the edges as I pushed my thoughts at him. *And last night did not prove otherwise.*

Ryu's eyes burned, smoke coming from his nostrils but he didn't respond.

Stopping a foot away from me, Ryu bent his head down to me. "How do I know you were not sent as a spy for that betrothed of yours?" What would he think about you kneeling for a drake?

I opened my mouth to retort and then thought better of it with the other two princes in the room. "How do you know about my betrothed?"

Ryu's gaze shifted to my handmaiden and I scowled at her. Someone else had loose lips as well.

Turning my attention back to the drake king, I stared those yellow green eyes down. *Prince Callahan has his own preferences and I have mine.*

Ryu's eyes trailed over my body, lingering over the places where the scars laid beneath the material. *And the markings? Are those your preference or his?*

I slapped him.

Everyone startled and jumped to their feet at the action. Ryu's face hadn't even turned at the action, his gaze showing no response as if it had not fazed him.

I wished I could say the same. My hand stung as much as the tears I refused to shed burned my eyes.

The brothers stepped up to either side of Ryu. The drake king held his hand up stopping them from intervening.

"My apologies, princess." Ryu inclined his head to me. "I should not have said that."

My lip curled up into a sneer, the fiery rage in my chest urging me to do more than slap the man beast.

A soft hand touched my elbow, and my eyes shifted reluctantly away from the drake king to Aryn. She stroked my arm and down the length of my hair, until the rage in me quelled to an ember. I let out a long breath, closing my eyes for a moment, a reminder to myself what was at stake here. My pride and honor could stand to be bruised and beaten for the sake of my people.

"Apology accepted." I inclined my head to the drake king, then scanned the faces of the two drakes at his side.

Ryu noticed my gaze shifting to the drakes and stepped back, gesturing to one and then the other. "These are my brothers. Ira."

I recognized one of them as the one who had taken me to Ryu's room last night. His good eye skimmed over me, a curious look making his brow rise.

"And Desmond." The other drake smiled as if something that we had said amused him.

Deciding now was as good a time as any to start gaining their favor, I lifted the sides of my crimson gown and gave them my best curtsey. I peered up at them beneath my long lashes offering them a coy smile. "A pleasure to meet you."

When I lifted from my curtsey, I had all eyes on me. I could feel the burn of their gazes on my chest pressed against the thin silken material. Just how I wanted it.

It riled something up in myself as well. Something I hadn't expected to feel with anyone other than a human man. Though after last night, I shouldn't be surprised that the attention of the two other drakes would cause a heat to build between my thighs.

The nostrils of the drakes' flared and I felt a sense of self satisfaction come over me.

Aryn stepped between us, a look of warning shooting my way before she gestured with her hands and her mouth so I could keep up. "You called for us, your majesty?"

I noticed the curious looks of the drake king's brothers at Aryn's hand movements but they didn't comment.

Ryu zeroed in on Aryn, his eyes noting her hand movements before answering in my mind as well as out loud.

"Since you will be with us for a while, I have decided you should become accustomed to our people and ways. My brothers," he inclined his head to Ira and Desmond in turn, "will be your escort through the caverns. I caution you not to leave their side," his serpentine eyes narrowed on me. "You will find that not all the drakes have love for our human brethren. Not even one as tempting as you, princess."

I licked my lips and shot a look at each of my new captors before stepping in close to the drake king. "And what of you? Why can't you be my guide?" I had to keep my thoughts to myself, knowing that the king and his brothers could very well skim from them what I planned. I had to be smart about this.

Of course the princess would only want Ryu.

Get used to it brother. Compared to the king we are nothing but tagalongs.

My brows shot up at the words filtering through my head. At my alarm, the drake king reached out with his own mind.

You will be safe with them.

As I am with you? I shot back with a scowl. Then cursed myself. I kept forgetting honey and not vinegar. How was I to get anywhere with them if I could not curb my need to fight back?

The drake king grabbed me by the back of the neck and dragged me close until I could feel the scorching heat of his breath on my face. *You are safe with me, little one. For how long, is up to you.*

With one last studious look, the drake king released me and signaled a hand to his brothers in some secret meaning. He gave me a pointed look with a growling voice in my head. *Behave.*

I resisted the urge to stick my tongue out at his back as he stalked out of the room. Instead, I refocused on the drakes before me.

"Well, gentlemen, I'm all yours." I crossed one arm under my breasts, shoving them up further and drawing the drakes' attention. My lips curled up at their reaction. This was going to be too easy.

Chapter 12

Ira

THE PRINCESS WAS NOT WHAT Ira had expected. He had heard of her beauty and grace. How she was loved by all her people and yet...

There was a fierceness in her that Ira could see that could only serve to endear her to them more. This was all in spite of or maybe because of her disability.

Ira stopped himself. His good eye shifted over to the dark head of the princess. He shouldn't say that.

While he had his own disabilities from the loss of his eye, he would never want anyone to think more or less of him because of it. It certainly didn't stop the princess from handing his brother, Ryu, his balls in a sack.

His lips ticked up at the thought, he stroked his chin and flicked his gaze over to his younger brother, Desmond. *Who do you think will win?*

Who? Desmond blinked at him in confusion.

You know who. The princess or our dear brother.

Desmond snorted.

The princess's handmaiden glanced over her shoulder at them with a curious frown.

If I know our brother, which I believe I do, then he will be bending over backwards for us to get rid of her within the week's end.

Ira shook his head. He'd thought the same thing when he first led the princess to his brother's bedroom. Then he met the actual princess. Now he pitied his brother for the headache he was surely facing with the princess in tow.

"Where are you taking us?" The handmaiden, Aryn, asked, stopping in the middle of the dirt and stone corridor. "We will not blindly follow you wherever you take us. How do we know you aren't taking us to our deaths?" The older woman scowled at us with her hands on her round hips.

The princess paused and turned to her handmaiden, her brows bunched together. Her hands flitted in front of her in rapid movements that Ira had a hard time keeping up with. Her handmaiden didn't have that problem. She shot a frown at them before returning the princess's hand movements with one of her own.

Ira leaned toward his brother "Do you know what they're doing?"

Desmond scratched the side of his face with his clawed finger. "Some kind of hand speech? I don't know. Humans are strange."

Pursing his lips, Ira tried to read the gestures but was at a loss. Without thinking much about it, he slipped into the princess's mind.

Why was she making things so difficult? We have no choice but to trust them. She was going to ruin everything!

Switching to the mind of Aryn, Ira growled at what he heard.

These savages are going to kill us if we don't escape first. I don't know why I even let myself get talked into this.

Thankfully, Desmond came to the rescue before Ira could say something that would only make matters worse.

"Ryu said to show you around. So that's what we're going to do." Desmond pushed between the humans and took the lead. "First stop, the marketplace. Now come on before you get left behind and believe me when I say that we are the nice ones."

Aryn glowered at Desmond's back and then gestured to the princess as if to say, "See."

The princess shook her head and followed after Desmond barely throwing a look my way.

Ira let out a long irritated breath before following after them. This couldn't get much worse.

They walked a bit further down the corridor before it opened up into a large cavern. This was the heart of the mountain. While the rest of drakes' home was broken up into winding corridors with small rooms here and there, the throne room and market place were the two main open areas, the market place the bigger of the two.

Ira had never been to a human marketplace but he would like to think their market place with the expansive stalls of goods and foods available were

149

better than anything the humans had to offer.

Ira almost bumped into the back of the princess who had stopped in the middle of the walkway to stare. He tried to see the market as she would for the first time.

Rows and rows of stalls lined the area with a large eating section placed in the middle. Here they would have performances or celebrations. Not that there had been much to celebrate as of late. Still, Ira watched as the princess's head jerked this way and that, taking in the nearby stalls. Before he could stop her, she darted over to a stall selling jeweled combs and the like.

The awe on her face was adorable as she fingered each thing in turn. Ira found himself smiling in spite of himself.

The drakes working the stalls watched the princess with a mixture of curiosity and disdain. If any of them planned to say something they took one look at Ira and Desmond and reconsidered, reluctantly allowing the human princess to have her way with their belongings.

She's a fascinating little thing, isn't she?

Ira shot a look at Desmond, arching a brow. *She certainly has a certain appeal.*

Yes, she does. I can see why our brother has become taken with her.

It sounds more like you're the one taken with her. Ira jerked his head toward the princess.

Desmond growled in response.

A shout and roar pulled their attention from the princess. While the market might be his favorite place in the mountain, it didn't exist without its fault.

So many drakes in one place would certainly cause friction between personalities. Sometimes that required them to step in and intervene.

Ira shot a look at Aryn and said, "Stay here."

A crash had Desmond and Ira rushing to the other side of the marketplace. He kept an ear out for any trouble that might head the princess's direction as he came upon two drake quarreling.

"What is the meaning of this?" Desmond snarled, stepping between the two drakes before they could cause more damage.

The first drake, one who went by the name Kayda, hardly looked at Desmond before glaring at the other drake. "He's a cheat. A swindler. No better than the human trash."

Ira tensed, glad the princess and her handmaiden were not in hearing distance.

"You take that back!" The second drake shouted, one whose name eluded Ira at the moment. "I make an honest living. My armors are genuine, strong as dragon fire and to say anything otherwise is a scourge upon my family name."

Ira inclined his head at the drake's words before looking to Kayda. "What proof do you have that what this drake says is not the truth?"

Kayda grabbed his bag and pulled out a chest plate. "I bought this from him two days ago and look at it." He tossed the broken and scorched plate on the ground. "It hardly lasted one bout in the rings before it cracked. Now tell me that is as strong as dragon's fire? I've seen turtle shells with more endurance."

Ira and Desmond exchanged a look.

What do you think?

Desmond shrugged. Who knows? To the crowd Desmond asked, "Can anyone vouch for this drake's armor?"

When no one immediately stepped forward, the drake tried to argue, "I told him that armor is not for fighting. It's more decorative."

"Why would you sell decorative armor?" Desmond sneered, stalking over to the drake's stall. He picked up one piece of armor and then another. He tapped a claw on a brace and then glanced over at Ira with an arched brow.

Ira jerked his head in a go-ahead motion.

Desmond's chest grew bright, a flame lighting from within. A few close drakes stepped back in preparation. Fire shot out of Desmond's jaws, completely encompassing the bracer and then became nothing but ash. It filtered through his fingers as he sent a pointed look at Ira.

Ira stepped forward and addressed the drake in question. "You will return his coin and find another way to make your living."

The drake snarled in Ira's face. "You can't do this. I'll take this to the king."

Ira grabbed the drake by the neck and jerked him forward until their noses bumped. "When you speak to me or my brother you are speaking to the king. Now do you want to lose your life as well as your business?"

The drake shook his head, defiance in his eyes.

"Good." Ira dropped him and stepped back. "Now why don't you clear —"

A scream pierced the air and all the drakes turned in one. The guilty drake scurried away before Ira could finish with him.

Desmond and Ira exchanged a look before darting through the crowd, pushing drakes out of the way as they went. They finally reached the center of the commotion and rage engulfed Ira.

In the center stood three drakes, each of whom Ira knew to be of less than reputable reputation, known for starting fights and general discourse in their home. They leered over Aryn and the princess. Aryn having been the one who screamed by the way she was carrying on.

The princess glowered at the drake holding her by the back of her hair, his hands groping at her clothing.

Vescera.

Vescera was the worst of them, he was one strike away from being killed. Ira thought his brother, Ryu, had been too lenient on the drake. He should have taken him out far sooner. With the state of it now, Vescera would be lucky if he received a swift death.

"What's a little mouse like you doing in the middle of the drake fortress?" Vescera cooed, stroking the side of her face. "Couldn't deal with the sad excuse for a cock offered to you by the humans?" He laughed and smiled at his friends. "Well, I can help you there." He leaned in closer to the princess and muttered something in her ear. The drake was obviously oblivious to the princess's condition.

Should we stop him?

Ira held his hand up. *No. Wait. I want to see what she does.*

Desmond shook his head. *Ryu will not be pleased.*

Probably not, but Ira wanted to see how the princess thought. Would she pass out and whimper like the lady she seemed to make everyone believe or would she fight back?

Vescera pulled back and frowned at the princess. The reaction he expected from her not coming. He shook her and growled, "What's wrong with you, little mouse? Are you broken?"

Ira knew she had understood what Vescera said this time.

The drake was far too interested in joking with his friends to notice the way the princess's eyes narrowed and her jaw clenched.

A strangled sound came out of her mouth that took a moment for Ira to realize it was her warrior sound before her leg swung up and collided with the drake's balls. He grunted and his grip on her loosened as he fell to the ground. Wrenching herself free, the princess spat on the drake kneeling before her, his hands clutching his sack.

Vescera's friends laughed, making no move to help him.

Should we step in now? Desmond asked impatience in his words.

Aryn came up beside the princess and quickly signed to her. The princess's eyes lit with a renewed fire and her leg swung out again, this time her foot catching the drake in the face.

This time his friends did not laugh, moving toward her with heavy growls.

Now.

Before Desmond and Ira could step in there was a roar loud enough to shake the mountain and the crowd parted for Ryu to come forth.

"What is the meaning of this?"

Chapter 13

A SENSE OF RELIEF SWEPT over me that surprised even me. Seeing the drake king should have irritated me or at least made me anxious. Except with the threat of the drakes before me imminent seeing Ryu only made me want to collapse to my knees.

At the drake king's appearance the crowd scattered. The two drakes who were seconds away from attacking me tried to sneak out as well but were caught by Ira and Desmond, who miraculously appeared from nowhere.

Ryu stalked forward, his gaze locking onto me and then onto the two drakes in his brothers' clutches and finally down to the drake on the ground.

The drake was out cold and couldn't do anything to defend himself. Satisfaction crept up inside of me.

"What happened?" Ryu asked, directing his words to his brothers. "You were supposed to be guarding her."

Desmond's shoulders hunched over while Ira's good eye lazily took in his brother.

I shifted my position so I could understand what they were saying better. Aryn grasped a hold of my arm, her body shaking so much that I feared she would faint.

"We were only gone for a moment," Desmond tried to explain, his face twisted in regret. "We didn't think anyone would try anything."

Ryu gestured at the three drakes with a flash of his fangs. "And yet they did."

The drake in Ira's grasp tried to struggle, his mouth moving frantically. "Didn't know she was taken."

The other in Desmond's grasp surged forward as well, seeing his opening to get out of trouble. "Yeah, not our fault. She isn't marked. How were we to know?"

Ryu's gaze shot to the drake on the ground before sliding up to my face. He took a step toward me and sniffed the air. Whatever he smelled made his jaw tighten and his chest flare that white orange light.

His eyes locked on mine as he spoke, "I will deal with you two later. It seems I have a situation to remedy." He took a step toward me, glanced down at the drake at his feet and added on, "Confine them. They'll pay for touching what is mine."

The single word sent a shiver through my body.

Ryu grabbed me by the wrist and pulled me forward. His touch scorched my skin and a gasp fell from me. He jerked me toward him and then wrapped an arm around my waist, throwing me over his shoulders.

Surprised and outraged, I beat on his back, digging my nails into whatever part of him I could get a hold of. A slap on my ass and a word of *Behave* filtered through my mind. The drakes around us watched from the sidelines none of them moving an inch to help me. I jerked my head up to see Aryn but she was already gone with Desmond and Ira.

I bounced on his back as he stalked down the corridors, his tail swayed behind me with each step. I glared at it. I didn't know where we were going or what his plans were and I wasn't sure I wanted to. What I did know was that he needed to put me down and now.

I shoved my thoughts at him with all my might. *Put me down you monstrous brute.*

Ryu jostled me and replied, *Not yet. Behave or I will show you what happens to little princesses who refuse to obey orders.*

A choked laugh came out of my throat. Obey. I hardly could say I have ever obeyed anyone in my life. Perhaps when I was a child and was threatened with a swatting. The thought made my lips curve up.

We came to a jerking halt and my head banged against Ryu's back.

"Watch it!"

Ryu ignored me and kicked in the door. One glance around the room told me we were back in his bedroom. My breath caught in my throat at the meaning behind it. What was he going to do? What did he mean he had a situation to remedy?

A few more bumpy steps and then I was tossed onto the bed. I gaped up at the drake king. "What do you think you're doing?"

Ryu's eyes darkened at my words.

Without a word, he grabbed the bottom of my skirt and pushed it up my thighs. I scrambled back from him, my heart hammering in my chest.

Now? Now he wants to bed me? I wasn't ready. I'm the one who was supposed to bed him, not the other way around.

I kicked my legs out and crawled across the bed, trying to get away from him. This wasn't going to work if he's the one claiming me. No. I had to be the one in control. Me.

A hand latched onto my ankle and dragged me back across the bed on my belly. A cry came out of my throat and I grabbed for the side of the bed. Ryu was stronger. He pushed me up onto my knees, my dress thrown over my hips baring my core to his view. Holding my legs open with his hands, something slid between my thighs and I jerked away from it.

I won't be fucked like some beast. I shouted at him in my mind.

The thing moved between my thighs again, slipping over my most sensitive area. A heat built at the touch and I twisted to see. I expected to see Ryu's cock getting ready to penetrate me but what I found instead was his tail toying with my heat. My breath escaped me in a rush as it slid over me once more, Ryu's hands on my thighs clenching and unclenching with each swipe of the tip of his tail.

What was he doing? Was this some kind of monstrous foreplay? Something to bring me mewling to his will because it was working.

My legs quivered beneath me as the tail found its rhythm. Pressure grew between my thighs and I knew that I wouldn't be able to hold it back much longer. Did he mean to break me before he fucked me?

Anger swept through me and I grit my teeth. I would not have it. I tried to focus on anything else. Anything that would lower the building pressure inside of me. Bogs weed. Three days old porridge. Cal's slimy hands on my flesh.

The tail disappeared. I thought I had held out long enough for him to get bored and relaxed. That was a mistake.

Ryu's hands drew my hips up and a hot wet muscle slipped between my folds. I cried out and struggled to get away. No. Yes. Fuck. This wasn't how it was supposed to go!

My fingers dug into the blankets beneath me, my eyes squeezing shut with every swipe of his tongue. It circled my clit, rotating around before flicking up and down my folds. It was so hot. Much hotter than any human tongue I'd ever had on me. It made each touch even more intense.

Ryu laved at me over and over again until I couldn't hold back anymore. All I could think about was more. I wanted more. Needed it. But Ryu never strayed into my hot canal. Not once did he penetrate me, his mouth focused solely on eating every bit of what was available on the outside. It was maddening. It was torture. It was oh so good.

My body tensed up readying itself to explode. A sharp pain to my inner thigh startled me but only caused my orgasm to come crashing down on me harder than it ever had before. My legs quaked beneath me, threatening to give out. I didn't have to worry, Ryu held on to me through all of it, his tongue lapping at my center until I collapsed my front half onto the bed, completely spent and ready to sleep.

With one final lick of my juices, Ryu released me, allowing my hips to lower down to the bed. He readjusted my skirt so that I was covered and started for the door.

I rolled over onto my side and watched him. "That's it?"

I was too spent to try and push my thoughts at him. Though, I was sure my voice wasn't exactly the sexiest thing he would want to hear after something like what he just did.

Ryu paused at the door and twisted to the side so I could see his face, his lips moving precisely with each word. "I meant what I said. I will not bed you until you are willing."

I arched my brow. "I do not think we have the same definition of bedding because that felt a lot like it to me."

Lips ticked up at one side, Ryu's gaze slid over my liquified form. "That was a marking. Now no other male will come near you. Believe me, when I bed you, you will know. Now sleep."

I frowned at his back as he left the room, closing the door behind him. A marking? What's that?

Then I remembered the sharp pain at the end. Gathering up my strength, my arms a bit wobbly as I lifted myself up, I pulled my skirt up and peered down at the place on the inside of my thigh where a perfect set of teeth marks lay just inches from my still aching core.

Scowling at the mark, I tossed my skirt back down and fell back on the bed with a sigh. Beastly, indeed.

Chapter 14

Ryu

THE HALBERT IN HIS HAND was heavy today. Claws wrapped tightly around the handle, Ryu swung it with all his might at the training dummy cutting the straw creature in half. The half not still attached to the pole fell to the ground in a scatter of golden pieces.

Three days. Three days of that incessant woman milling about his home, charming his guards, his brothers, and anyone else she could sink her claws into.

It was bad enough that the males were falling all over themselves to please her, even the women were delighted by her presence.

So much for his warning. Ryu lined up another dummy to begin swinging at again. He'd been working at it all morning. Ever since he woke up next to the princess, curled around her like some dragon with his horde, like she belonged to him. Ridiculous.

Not that she helped matters much. Making those small sounds in her throat while she slept, her tiny fingers curled around whatever part of him she could grab, those legs thrown over his waist.

His damnable tail was a traitor. It wanted nothing more than to slip around her hips and slide between her thighs once more. Ryu could still taste her on his tongue.

He sliced the dummy in half again. Ryu swung the halbert around, going through the motions of the training instilled in him since a young child.

Marking someone as his was supposed to keep the other drakes away from her. Scream for all to hear that she belonged to him. It hadn't done what he expected.

Sure it kept the male drakes from trying to mate with her again but it had not been enough to keep them completely away. Ryu would just have to find another way to keep them from her.

He tried not to think too deeply on the reasoning behind wanting to keep her all to himself. It wasn't like he cared for the human female. She was the enemy and up to something, he could feel it. Even if she has guarded her thoughts so closely that he couldn't make out horns or tails on what she was planning.

He supposed he could get the information from her handmaiden, Aryn. She seemed far more easy to read than the princess. Aryn also didn't seem to have that stubbornness or bite the princess flaunted in his face at every turn. Ryu swore she was more dragon than most of the drakes here.

"I knew we would find him in here," Desmond's voice sounded through the training cavern. Ryu let his eyes slide over to his brothers, not letting up on the swings of his weapon. "How long have you been in here?"

Ryu grunted and stabbed the empty air before him. "Long enough that my advisors are probably complaining about me being late again."

Ira watched him with a studious gaze not saying anything. He might have lost one of his eyes but it didn't keep him from seeing far more than he should.

Ryu lowered the halbert and turned to his brothers, a scowl on his face. "What?"

Desmond exchanged a look with Ira and then stepped forward, picking up a sword from the rack of them along the wall. "We are just concerned for you." He positioned himself in a fighting stance across from Ryu and gestured for Ryu to come at him.

Not one to give up the chance for an actual sparring partner, no one wanted to fight the king these days, Ryu lifted his halbert up ready for an attack. Desmond came at him fast, his feet moving so quickly that Ryu had a hard time keeping track of them. His brother had always been that way though. Quick on his feet and even quicker to speak what he shouldn't.

"Georgia is getting to you," Desmond stated, dipping around him and almost catching him on the back but Ryu's tail swiped out at the last second knocking it away.

"Georgia, now is it?" Ryu growled, swung the halbert over his head and then down across the front of Desmond. His brother jumped back and came at him with his sword, it clashed against the handle of his weapon and they were face to face in a struggle for dominance.

"That is her name, isn't it?" Desmond bit back at him, baring his teeth in a cheeky grin. "Perhaps, if you spent more time getting to know the princess and less time grumbling and trying to keep everyone else away from her you would see that she's not so bad."

Ryu shoved with all his might, pushing Desmond back and swung his tail and halbert at the same time. Desmond dodged the first but got hit across the chest by the other, knocking him to his knees, Ryu's weapon pressed up against the side of his neck.

"I have other matters to focus on than a human princess with a death wish."

Desmond snorted. "If you think that woman has a death wish then you haven't been paying close enough attention. If anything she just needs a good solid dick or three —" he waggled his brow at Ryu and then Ira "— to loosen her right up and all that fire in her will turn to a melted puddle in your hand."

"I have no intentions of bedding the princess." Ryu jerked his weapon away from his brother with a huff, shooting them a warning look. "And neither should either of you."

Desmond arched a brow and smirked. "Then what was the point of marking her as yours?"

"Yes," Ira finally spoke up from his place on the sideline. "What was the reasoning behind your marking the female? You haven't marked a single one since you came into maturity and yet you mark this one? This human female that you claim you do not want to bed and yet won't send away?"

"Sounds like someone is lying to themselves," Desmond chuckled and swung the sword in front of him a few good times. "Perhaps it is you that needs to be fucked. Get her out of your system and then maybe we can find out why she is really here."

Ryu growled low in his chest, not bothering to answer as he turned from his brothers, finding his mug of ale on the nearby table. He downed a good portion of it before swiping his face with the cloth, wiping away the lingering sweat and dirt from his training.

"I marked her because the other males would not leave her be if I hadn't," Ryu explained. "The last thing we need is the human females getting taken advantage of by our own. They have a bad enough opinion of us."

"And yet they haven't run..." Ira pointed out with a frown. "Do you not find that odd?"

Ryu shrugged one shoulder, the armor there clinking against itself. "Where would they run to? You know as well as I that this place is not much more than a maze to anyone who does not know its layout. And I have posted guards on them at all times. When would they have the chance?"

"I would not put it past them to find a way." Ira continued, moving toward Ryu with a deeper frown. "They found a way into our lair which we have kept secret for centuries. Is that not a strange coincidence?"

Ryu slid his tongue along one of his fangs and thought about what his brother said. Really thought about it. Were they being played? Had the princess put herself in harm's way on purpose?

"There's something else," Desmond began, taking a seat on the bench near him. "We have been getting reports of soldiers searching the woods."

Brow furrowed, Ryu asked, "Kinoko soldiers?"

Desmond shook his head. "I do not believe so. They don't have the same coloring or sigil. I would say they belong to

Georgia's betrothed — Prince Callahan — but they do not bear his markings either."

"Perhaps someone is trying to find the princess without letting anyone know who is looking for her?" Ira offered up as a suggestion. "Do we know if the king has made any kind of announcement in regards to her whereabouts?"

"Not as of yet," Demond continued and played with the rings lining his ear. "I would think they would keep her disappearance a secret until they have exhausted their resources. Especially with her marriage to the Plumus Prince so near. They would not want to alarm the people."

Ira snorted.

"You think otherwise?" Ryu prodded his brother, the more serious of the three.

Ira let his hands sit on his hip where his dagger sat, his fingers tight around the hilt. "I think we are being played but by who and to what end?"

"Maybe we should just give her back?" Desmond suggested with a wicked gleam in his eyes. "Bind her, blind fold her, and dump her and her handmaiden somewhere in the middle of the forest."

"And what if she tells her father or betrothed where we are hiding?" Ryu asked his arms over his chest trying to stanch the tight feeling that came from talking about giving her up. He didn't want her here. It shouldn't matter if she leaves then right? Apparently some part of him did not like that idea.

Desmond shrugged. "What's she going to say? We live underground? There are many caves and underground systems that the Kinokos are unaware of. It would take them ages to find us if at all. By then they will have long forgotten."

"While an optimistic plan, how do we even know she wants to go back?" Ryu countered with a slight uptick of his lips. "The one time the handmaiden had demanded their return, it seemed almost as if..." he paused, licking his lips as he recalled the look on the princess's face, the pure horror of the suggestion. "...I'm not so sure returning them will work in either of our favors."

Ira cocked a brow. "Then what do you suggest we do? Wait and see what the princess does? See if her father or worse betrothed comes bearing down on us demanding we return her? She is more trouble than she's worth. And what exactly are we getting out of having her here anyway?"

Ryu let the air settle between them for a moment before he spoke. "I do not wish to do anything rash. If we send her back then we do not know what she came here for in the first place and I for one would like to know before the dagger swings at my back."

"Perhaps..." Ira began and then stopped almost second guessing himself.

"What?" Ryu urged.

Ira sighed and his good eye rolled up to the dirt and stone ceiling. "Perhaps, we test them. Find out if they are really here because they want to be or because they truly did venture too far into the woods."

"And how exactly do you propose we do that?" Desmond asked, intrigue on his face. Ryu could see where his brother was coming from. More information would be better than going in blindly waiting for the princess or her family to show their true hand.

"Aryn has complained about wanting to go outside," Ira stated, seemingly off topic. "Perhaps we take them to the nearby spring? Maybe when the soldiers we've spotted are nearby?" He stroked his chin with his clawed fingers. "Perhaps a few of the guards decide to give them privacy and they are left to their own devices?"

Ryu's lips curled up at the edges into a wicked smile. "Let us see where their loyalties truly lie. Either way we get our answer."

Chapter 15

I RUBBED AT THE MARK on my inner thigh, the spot still ached even three days later though it showed no signs of infections.

"Stop it." Aryn signed to me from my side in the female's quarters. Since the scene at the marketplace the drake king hadn't let me or Aryn roam anywhere but his bedroom and the females' quarters. I'd rather die than sit in his bedroom waiting for him to come back like a good little puppy dog waiting for a treat. I might be trying to seduce them but I wasn't desperate...not yet anyway.

I scowled at her, dropping my hand from my leg. I signed back to her. "It still hurts."

Aryn's nose scrunched up. "I would think so. He bit you."

I frowned, pursing my lips. "But why? It doesn't make any sense. Why would he bite me and..." I trailed off, my face heating at the memory of what else the drake king had done to me in the process of biting the inside of my thigh. "Anyway, it's making the females look at me strangely. The males — even the guards — won't come closer to me than they have to." Each movement of my hands grew more aggressive as I ranted.

Aryn's shoulders heaved as she blew out a breath. Her eyes skimmed over to Beautine, who helped a few other female drakes work on a clothing project. That seemed to be what most of the female drakes did all day. They worked on projects or talked amongst themselves, not to me, but to each other. Though, they were more likely to talk to Aryn it seemed.

I watched Aryn's mouth move as she called out to the drake. Beautine's head turned, her gorgeous locks falling over her shoulders as she shifted to come closer to us.

"Yes?" Beautine's lovely mouth moved in the shape of the words, her gaze sliding from Aryn to me. "Is there something you need?"

Aryn shifted in place and shot me a look before explaining to Beautine the problem moving her hands at the same time for me.. "I was hoping you could explain why the drake king would mark the princess. It's causing her quite the distress."

Beautine arched a brow at me and then turned back to Aryn. Her mouth moved quickly and I narrowed my eyes on her lips trying to catch what she was saying though, I caught only a few of the words. Mark. Males. Claim. Each word made my eyes narrow further and my jaw tighten.

I waved a hand to get Aryn's attention, signing to her slowly. "He marked me so the other males would stay away?"

Aryn grimaced and nodded.

A growl reverberated from my chest and I jumped to my feet. I stalked to the door, planning on confronting Ryu for what he did to my person and without my permission. I'd had quite enough men marking up my body for their own enjoyment, he would not be another one of them. I was in control here. Not him.

I jerked open the door and barreled to a stop, Aryn bumped into my back. I shot her a scowl over my shoulder and then glared up at the drake king who blocked the doorway.

The drake king took one look at me and commanded in my mind, *Come.* He turned on his heel and strode down the hallway as if I were some kind of dog for him to command. I glowered at his back and then glanced over at Aryn who only shrugged.

Not wanting to give into the drake king's command but needing to speak with him, I hurried down the hall after him, ignoring the looks I received from the two menacing guards by the doorway.

Aryn clung to my arm as we made our way down the hallway. I didn't know if the command included her or not but I wouldn't leave her behind. I scrambled up to the side of the drake king, grabbing his arm before he could lose us in the tunnels.

Ryu glanced down at my hand but didn't shake it off. Lifting those yellow green eyes to mine, Ryu lifted a brow, an unspoken question to my actions.

Where are we going? I asked in my mind and with my hands. Then without signing I added on in my head. *You had no right to mark me. I don't belong to* you.

The drake king flashed me a fanged smile. *The mark on you says otherwise.* He leaned toward me not caring that Aryn was standing right there. Tipping my chin up with a clawed finger, he brushed his nose along the line of my jaw. *Didn't you offer yourself to me? I do not like others touching what is mine.*

If Cal or Lou had said those things I would have stiffened, become nauseous, and wanted to run away. There was something about Ryu. Something about how he touched me, how he looked at me, the way he made sure that I came before he put his mark on me made everything completely different. The thought of belonging to him didn't disgust me. It didn't make me want to run away screaming. It made my blood rush south and my nipples harden. It made me want to roll over on the ground like a cat and spread myself before him so he could do it all over again.

I licked my suddenly dry mouth and pulled away from his touch. I ignored the heated look Ryu gave me and refocused on why he had told me to follow him in the first place.

Where are we going?

Ryu dropped his hand and said out loud, "My brother has informed me that you wish to go outside."

My eyebrows rose and I chanced a look at Aryn. I hadn't mentioned anything about going outside. The way Aryn practically vibrated with excitement answered my own question. Seems like I hadn't been paying enough attention to my handmaiden as of late. I didn't realize she had been so miserable underground.

I lifted my chin and stared Ryu down. "Well, let's go."

Ryu led us down several pathways, winding back and forth so that we would never find our way back on our own. And that was probably the point. The drake king didn't want us to know how to get back. Could this be a trick?

The drake king glanced over his shoulder at me and I scrambled to keep my mind blank. If this was a trick then I didn't want to give the drake king anything to use against us. Think of nothing. Think of boring topics. The walls....they were boring. Brown and gray. Nothing interesting about them at all. I couldn't even think about them at length, there was simply nothing to say about them.

My gaze slipped to the drake king's back. His red hair trailed down the back of his head, ending at just the top of his back. My eyes slid over the bare muscles of his yellowish gold skin marveling in the way the torch light glinted off the scales sprinkling along each plane of flesh until I reached his tail. Thick at the base and thinning out until it reached the end, it blocked what little the cloth around his waist covered of his buttocks.

I remember feeling those muscular thighs beneath my hands as my mouth devoured his length. I wondered if he was as savage and aggressive with his love making as he was when he came in my mouth, his hot seed spilling down my throat and chin. It had been empowering to cause such a strong beast to tremble under my actions.

Ryu jolted to a stop and I almost ran into his back. Pulling back sharply, I glowered at his back before he spun around on us. His mouth moved and I missed what he said as he addressed Aryn.

Aryn's hand clutched my arm and then looked from me to Ryu and then back again.

I gestured to her, "What is it?"

"He wants to take you alone first." She paused and swallowed before continuing, "He doesn't trust that we won't run off together. He will take you first and then me so we have to stay or risk leaving the other behind."

My eyes narrowed on her hands and then shot to Ryu, a scowl covering my face. I shove my words at him venomously. *Do you trust us so little?*

Ryu's eyebrows arched and his lips ticked up. *I don't trust you at all. Be glad I am giving you this when I could have left you in a cell to rot.*

Resisting the urge to roll my eyes at his attempt at a power play, I nodded to Aryn before answering with my hands. "I'll be fine. Go back to the room."

Aryn gave me a worrying look once more before a nearby guard stepped in to escort her back to the female's quarters.

Then I was alone with the drake king once more.

I didn't know why my heart began to beat so rapidly. I slept by his side each night. We didn't touch each other, not like the first night I was brought to his bedroom or the time he marked me but we still laid together. I refused to acknowledge the way my body betrayed me during the night and wrapped itself around the drake king like he was the safest place I could be. I was simply drawn to the warmth of his body, that was all.

Ryu didn't wait for me to respond before he began walking again. I kept a few steps behind him, careful of his tail moving back and forth between us. One wrong move and I'd trip over it and fall face first into the drake king.

Thankfully, we didn't walk for much longer before the dim corridor brightened and the sunlight beamed down on us. I squinted at the light, lifting my hand to block the majority of it. Who knew that three days underground would cause the light to be so much brighter than before?

Once my eyes adjusted I searched around for where the drake king had brought me.

Trees lined the clearing just outside the entrance of the cave and a little beaten path led to a small pool of water where steam drifted up into the air in curls. The bright blue sky cast across the sky where the canopy opened up above the spring. If I could still hear, I bet even the bird would be chirping a happy little song.

I gaped at the perfect hot spring and then went back to Ryu. *Why?*

Ryu prowled toward me with a hungry glint in his eyes.

Licking my lips, I tangled my hands into my skirts and backed away from him.

Run.

Chapter 16

GATHERING MY SKIRTS IN MY hands, I spun on my heel and ran toward the pool of hot water. I had no idea where I was going or what I was doing but the heated look in the drake king's eyes told me that I needed to play along. Because this was someone I wanted to catch me.

A delicious shudder went through me at what might happen if and when the drake king caught me.

The ground vibrated beneath my feet and my back warmed with each inch Ryu gained on me. My feet dragged to a stop in front of the spring, my eyes darting around the clearing. Unless I wanted to go traipsing through the woods there was nowhere left to go.

Turning to face my fate, I locked my gaze with the prowling drake. His tail slid from side to side on the ground, his footsteps steady as they came toward me. Putting a confident smirk on my face, I took the only action I could in this situation.

I stripped.

My heart pounded in my chest as my fingers curled around the holds of my top. Keeping my eyes locked on the drake king, who had slowed his progress, I untied my top and let it drop to the ground, baring my breasts to the open air and Ryu's gaze.

My chest lifted and fell in quick succession the longer Ryu stared at my face. I wish he would just look already. See the scars. My stomach rolled with anxiety waiting to see the look of disgust on his face.

After what seemed like forever, Ryu came to a stop a few feet away from me. Those chartreuse eyes drifted from my face and down my neck to linger over my heaving breasts. I lifted my chin higher the longer his gaze lingered.

Who?

The single growling question reverberated through my head, making me wince.

My hands moved up to cover myself but Ryu was suddenly there holding my wrists and keeping my arms down.

Who did this to you?

I licked my lips, my eyes looking off at the woods rather than to see the pitying expression that was surely on his face. Swallowing down the bile that rose in my throat, I forced myself to meet his gaze.

The heat that had been in his eyes before had turned molten for a completely different reason. One that sent a chill down my spine and not for a good reason.

Ryu's claws traced along the swell of my breasts and then found the edge of the first scar just above my heart. The touch of his claw was gentle but firm and I wanted him to stop focusing on my scars and start focusing on other parts of me.

Flicking my hair over my shoulder, I grabbed the folds of my skirt and pulled them loose. It fell to the ground leaving me naked except for the slippers on my feet. I kicked them off and stepped back from the drake who was still glowering at the scars maring my flesh.

Do not walk away from me, female.

Letting my lips tug up at the edges, I walked backward until my feet touched the hot spring. I inched back, my eyes lingering on the drake king while I let the water envelope me. The heat covered my body hiding away the marks on my skin from the drake king's lingering gaze.

Tell me.

I pursed my lips. *A woman bares herself to you and all you can focus on is the marks. If I hadn't had you in my mouth I would think you were not interested...*

I let my fingers trail over my breast bone and cupped my breasts with both hands, pinching my nipples just so that a hard breath escaped me and my eyes fluttered shut. I let my other hand slip down my waist and in between my thighs.

The water lapped against me and a hand grabbed my wrist stopping me from touching myself where I ached the most.

My eyelids flipped open and I locked eyes once more with the drake king. Since he was a foot or more taller than me the water stopped at his waist, his tail making the water ripple with each movement.

Didn't I already prove this to you? He leaned in closer until I could feel the heat of his breath on my face. *I don't like anyone touching what belongs to me.*

Ryu dragged me forward until my nipples scraped against the rough surface of his chest. He'd completely stripped his armor off and the hard press of his length

187

against my stomach told me he was just as naked as me.

Placing my hands on his chest, I slid them up and around his shoulders fingering the hair at the nape of his neck. Those clawed fingers fingered my waist and hips watching and waiting for me to make the next move.

I had an idea.

I pulled my lower lip between my teeth and inched my fingers up until I found the edges of Ryu's horns. His breath blew out against my face and his chest rumbled against mine making my nipples sing.

Careful, female. There is no going back after this.

My mouth went dry at his words and I reminded myself everything that was at risk. The very reason I was there. I had to do this. And if I was being honest with myself, I wanted to do this.

I wanted to know what it was like to have his tongue and fangs on every inch of me. To feel him between my thighs, his chest growing red with that inner light as he came inside of me.

Ryu was right. There was no going back after this. Once I crossed this line...

Not letting myself ponder it any longer, I wrapped my fingers around each of the horns on his head stroking them up and down as I had done with his long hard cock days ago.

Ryu's hips bucked against my stomach, his claws biting into my flesh. Something wrapped around my waist lifting me up, my legs spread and grasped him between them, his tail holding me in place while his hands gripped my backside. Now his length slid against my aching core. Hot and hard it slipped between my folds, pressing against my throbbing bundle of nerves.

Ryu pulled us up and out of the spring, my hands moving along the length of his horns enjoying every rumble of his chest the faster I moved them.

The world tilted and I found myself falling, the drake king came with me until my back pressed against the soft damp grass at the edge of the hot spring.

Ryu's head lowered, his mouth finding my own as his cock bumped against my core once more. That tongue lapped at my lips, nipped at my tongue before develing inside to take over my mouth. He tasted hot and smoky against my tongue. It was so different from anyone I'd ever been with before.

Stop thinking about other males. His growling voice thrust into my head the way I wanted him to thrust into my body.

I arched my hips up, trying to drag him closer.

So impatient. He released my lips and nudged my chin with his nose, his hands holding himself up over me. That tail of his teased me between my legs opening me up for him as he settled his length at my opening.

I held my breath. My eyes found Ryu's. He surged forward, stretching and filling me up until I felt like I might burst. I grabbed something, anything, to hold on to. I found his horns again and Ryu stiffened.

My breathing came out in long pants as I adjusted to his length. I wiggled against him, urging him to start moving.

His hips drew back until he was almost completely out of me before he surged forward once more hitting somewhere deep inside of me. A dull ache began to grow, a swelling of pleasure that threatened to overflow as I held on for dear life.

Ryu gripped my hips and lifted me off the ground, the angle making him go in deeper and harder.

Something tickled at my backside and my back stiffened.

Relax.

The purr of Ryu's voice in my head made my body ease up and the thing that

I now realized was his tail inched between my butt cheeks. I sucked in a breath as it teased my back hole, easing in and then out adding just a little bit more with each thrust.

If I thought I was full before now I was bursting at the seams. Anymore and I would explode into a million pieces.

Ryu's claw stroked my bundle between my thighs and that was enough to send me over the edge. My throat ached at the savage scream that barreled out of me. Birds burst out of the trees around us, scattering across the sky. I'd have been embarrassed by my outburst if I could feel anything outside of the quivers that kept going through me as my orgasm lingered.

A hot heat burned against my chest, a bright red light filling Ryu's chest, and then scorching strings of seed coated the inside of my womb.

When the quiver finally stopped I let out a long breath and sighed happily up at the drake king. Ryu leaned back, his length and tail pulling out of me, making me feel empty and hollow.

I leaned up on my elbows watching him as he turned to the hot spring and washed himself. My eyes caught on something on the ground. I glanced to the side and found five long gouges on either side of me, digging into the ground and leaving glowing scorch marks in their wake.

Humming to myself, I pushed onto my knees and searched for my skirt. Without Ryu's hot form against me it was getting chilly.

Here.

I peered up at him from beneath my lashes, something in me suddenly becoming shy even after he'd been inside every part of me.

Ryu lifted me up and walked us into the hot spring. When the warm water touched my still sensitive parts, I let out a hiss of breath. Ryu slid his fingers gently between my folds and butt cheeks, cleaning me off before stepping back to look down at me.

We should — his words in my head cut off as his head jerked to the side, angling to the side. His lips pressed together tightly and his eyes narrowed. *Wait here.*

Frowning at his back, I sunk further into the hot spring. I didn't know what caught the drake king's attention but I didn't want to be caught naked and unaware.

When Ryu didn't return right away, I inched onto the shore once more and scrambled for my clothes. I grabbed the skirt around me, my eyes searching the woods for Ryu's familiar face.

A hand grabbed my shoulder and jerked me around.

I came face to face with Mushion, the head of the Kinoko's guard. His mouth moved quickly, his eyes darting from side to side. Behind him his soldiers waited along the lines of the woods, their swords out and at the ready.

I waved my hand at him, gesturing for him to slow down. What was he doing here? They had to leave before Ryu got back.

Mushion paused and slowly tried to sign to me what he wanted. Not everyone in the kingdom knew the hand movements but it meant something that he tried.

"You. Me. Leave. Come." He grabbed my elbow and tried to pull me to my feet.

I held my skirt up against my body, hiding my nudity from the others and pulled back from him with a shake of my head.

"Why?" He said aloud his mouth forming the word as he frowned.

I licked my lips and tried to figure out how to explain. How did I tell them what was going on? How did I explain? Would they even believe me? I glanced down at my nakedness and thought for just a second about showing them. Giving them real proof of what the prince and his brother were like but the thought of showing them made my insides roll with sickness. Instead, I said, "I can't leave yet."

"They're monsters," Mushion said, his jaw clenching tight and his eyes filled with hatred. Just like everyone else who thought about the drakes. "Why would you want to stay?"

I opened my mouth to answer him.

Yes. Please enlighten me, princess. I spun around to see Ryu standing in the clearing. *Why won't you leave with them?*

Chapter 17

Ryu

HOLDING BACK THE BEAST INSIDE of him was the hardest thing Ryu ever had to do. But standing there with so many males so close to the one he marked made it increasingly difficult, especially when she still had his scent all over her. A small part of him swelled with satisfaction.

The soldiers bearing the Kinoko's sigil, a dragon with its wings splayed as if about to take flight, decorating the front of the black and green armor. Perhaps they were friends with our ancestors at one point and adopted their symbol but friends they were no longer. The glaring hatred coming from each of the soldiers' faces said as much.

The Kinoko princess held her crimson skirt to her naked form. The blonde male inched closer to the princess, his armor marked different from the others. A low growl of warning rumbled from Ryu's chest at the male. The soldiers' gripped their sword hilts at the sound.

Ryu ignored them, stalking forward. The soldiers stiffened, a few of their gazes dipped down to his bare form. Humans and their prudish minds. Though, the way they were dipping their gazes to the princess's bare skin made Ryu wish that he had covered her up before he had taken to the woods.

Georgia clung to the fabric, her eyes wide and her heart beating so loud that Ryu could have heard it from the other side of Kinoko.

"Come, princess," the soldier at her side said and tried to pull her away again.

Again the princess refused, pushing his hands away from her. Her head shook again, her dark hair falling over her shoulders and hiding some of her nakedness.

Ryu snarled at the hand touching his property. "It seems the princess does not want to leave with you."

"What do you know?" the soldier scowled, pushing up to his feet. "You must have done something to her. Why else would she want to stay here with a monstrous beast like you?"

Ryu ignored the soldier's words and dipped into the princess's mind. The thoughts raced across her mind and were almost too fast for him to understand.

What am I going to do now?

I was just getting somewhere with the king and now they had to show up and ruin it all. Aryn is going to kill me if this ends up being all for nothing.

His eyes zeroed in on the princess and her mind went blank.

"It seems like we are at an impasse, human." Ryu announced, stepping closer to the princess. "You may want to take her but I am not so sure I want to let her go."

The soldier tried to grab the princess again and Georgia jerked away from him the material falling to the ground between them, leaving the princess exposed to their prying eyes. Ryu let out a snarl and grabbed for her, sweeping her up into his arms and pushing her behind him.

Eyes wide with horror, the soldier unsheathed his sword, his fellow soldiers following suit as he demanded, "What did you do to her?"

It took Ryu a moment to realize what the soldier was talking about. Ryu peered at the princess behind him, her hands gripping his arm to her. The way the princess clung to him made a possessive part of Ryu gleam with pride.

"I did not harm your princess."

"Likely story, you drake scum," the soldier pointed his sword at Ryu's chest, his men closing in around him. "Let her go or you will have the whole of the Kinoko kingdom as well as her betrothal's kingdom stalking at your doorstep."

The princess curled around Ryu's arm and said in that muted tone of hers, "Mushion, I am not under some spell."

This Mushion man glanced from Ryu to the princess and tried to gesture to her the way her handmaiden did but gave up halfway through when he realized that he couldn't with his sword in his hand. Sighing, he shoved his sword back into its sheath and then tried again.

Not understanding what he was saying to the princess, Ryu slipped into the soldier's head with such ease that it was laughable.

What could the princess be thinking?

These creatures can't help us. The only one who can help us is her by marrying the prince.

The mention of the princess's betrothed reminded him of the marks on her body. The scars that covered her otherwise perfect skin with pale pink and raised lines. They were recent, not old scars. Ones that had only just begun to heal.

Ryu didn't need to dip into the princess's head to know the answer to his unanswered question. Rage filled Ryu's chest and smoke curled out of his nostrils. The soldiers stiffened and lifted their swords at the glow coming from Ryu's chest.

Georgia grasped his arm and rubbed it up and down, trying to soothe him.

"How can you be with this monster?" Mushion snarled, pointing a finger at Ryu.

Ryu had enough. He grasped the princess by the arm and turned her, pulling her arm up and over her head so they could see the word that curved along her ribs. He made sure to keep the silken cloth over the rest of her form as she trembled against him.

"Does this look like something a drake would do?" Ryu snarled at the soldiers. "We may be monsters but we at least treat our females with respect."

Mushion's eyes slid down to the still healing words carved into the princess's side and his eyes widened. Realization and horror dawned on his and every single soldiers' face.

Georgia jerked against his grasp and glowered at him as he released her, her nose red and her eyes glassy. *You had no right.*

I will not hand you over to male who would do this to you. Ryu gestured at her body a snort of heat coming from his nose. Then Ryu paused, his head cocked to the side and he stared down at her for a long moment.

That was it all along, wasn't it?

Why had it taken him so long to understand?

Ira had been right. This little princess hadn't gotten lost in the woods she had put herself there on purpose. All so she could get to him. Use him. Well, that would not do.

The princess backed away from him slightly, taking in his rumbling form.

You wished to seduce me, did you? Ryu purred in her head, a cruel grin curling up his face. *Well, it seems like you achieved that part of your plan.*

The princess held her skirt tightly to her figure, her fingers turning white with how hard she gripped the material.

Shaking her head, Georgia's throat bobbed as she swallowed. *It wasn't like that.*

Then what was it like, princess? He prowled toward her, while she backed up to her soldiers. They gave them strange looks, unable to figure out what was going on between them.

Georgia glanced at the soldiers and then back to Ryu again, her heart pounding even faster in her chest.

What would she do now that her plan had come to the surface? What had she expected to come of seducing him? Did she simply want to have a dangerous adventure before she married her sadistic betrothed?

Then she did something Ryu didn't expect.

Falling to her knees before him, the princess bowed her head and a slow sob escaped from her throat.

Ryu stiffened.

Crying. He could not stand crying.

Drake females did not cry. Or if they did they had the decency to do it behind closed doors. What was he supposed to do with a crying female?

Ryu shot a look at the soldiers who peered down at the princess with as much confusion as Ryu seemed to have.

The princess finally broke through her crying to answer him.

I can't go home. She sniffed and choked a sob. *You saw what he did to me. What he will continue to do until I am dead.*

Something tightened in Ryu's chest but he pushed it down. *How is that my problem?*

Her shoulders bunched up and then her sobbing stopped and her eyes lifted to his, a burning rage in them that would burn even a dragon's hide. *When Cal and his horrid brother come to hunt you down then will it be your problem?*

Ryu placed his hands on his hips and then walked around the kneeling princess. The soldiers watched him with cautious eyes but did not attack. Ryu picked up his loin cloth and wrapped it back around his waist. He then began putting on each piece of his armor in a slow precise fashion as he surveyed the group of humans in his territory.

His foot caught on the edge of the princess's top. He kicked it toward her with a sneer. "Your princess seems to be under the impression that I care about what happens to your kind. If you chose a monster —" he snorted a laugh — "for your future king, how is that my problem?"

Mushion's head jerked to the princess and then back to Ryu before back to the princess. He drew her attention and then gestured a few times to her. The princess glared at the soldier before gesturing back with a few violent motions before pointing at Ryu.

Do you think I am so dumb that I do not know you are talking about me?

Georgia snapped her glare at him. *You were dumb enough to think I could stumble upon your lair.*

Mushion cleared his throat and stepped toward Ryu. "The princess has informed me that in addition to the atrocities that have been thrust upon her by her betrothed, she and her handmaiden overhead..." he paused and frowned at the wording, "Found out that the Plumus prince plans to not only take over our kingdom but eradicate your kind from it."

Ryu adjusted the brace on his arm and stared down the soldier until he flinched and looked away. Then Ryu turned his attention back to the princess who slowly tried to dress herself without showing more of her scars to the soldiers. Just seeing a glimpse of them made the rage flare up inside of Ryu again.

"And what am I supposed to do about it? We drakes have survived for centuries.

Many of you have tried to remove us before and have not succeeded." Ryu's tail swung and hit the ground with a growl. "We will survive this coming storm as well."

"What about me?"

Ryu's eyes snapped to the princess as she stood to her feet. Her fingers curled into tight fists at her side as she walked toward him.

"I love my people as much as you love yours," her words came out stronger than any he had heard from her before, her face set in a determined scowl. "I have offered myself up to our enemy —" she locked eyes with him, the soldiers shifting in discomfort at her words, "—in hopes that you would see reason enough to help us, to help yourselves, to fight against this threat. But I see you are nothing more than cowards hiding under your mountain while the world passes you by." She stopped before him, shoving a finger at his chest. "You might survive for another century but your cowardice will be forever."

Fire burned in Ryu at not just her words but at the look in her eyes. So determined. So fierce. If the soldiers weren't there then Ryu would throw her down and take her all over again.

Ryu grabbed her around the waist, making the soldiers tense in reaction. His clawed hand cupped her chin and lifted it up to his. You wanted our help princess, you've got it. I hope you can handle it.

About the Author

Erin Bedford is an otaku, recovering coffee addict, and Legend of Zelda fanatic. Her brain is so full of stories that need to be told that she must get them out or explode into a million screaming chibis. Obsessed with fairy tales and bad boys, she hasn't found a story she can't twist to match her deviant mind full of innuendos, snarky humor, and dream guys.

On the outside, she's a work from home mom and bookbinger. One the inside, she's a thirteen-year-old boy screaming to get out and tell you the pervy joke they found online. As an ex-computer programmer, she dreams of one day combining her love for writing and college credits to make the ultimate video game!

Until then, when she's not writing, Erin is devouring as many books as possible on her quest to have the biggest book gut of all time. She's written over thirty books, ranging from paranormal romance, urban fantasy, and even scifi romance.

www.erinbedford.com